CHOGOLA CAPTIVE

Sergeant Guy DuBose struggled with the rawhide bonds that squeezed hard into the flesh of his wrists and arms. He lay off to one side of the Chogola camp where the warriors had thrown him—the war band, including a dozen Kiowa, numbered over a hundred.

A glance showed that the Indians had begun to drink. One man, the alcohol hitting him hardest, stood up and began singing a war song shuffling through a dance. Others joined until the Chogola version of a gala celebration was in full swing.

DuBose worked doubly hard with the slim strips binding his wrists. It hurt like hell as his skin rubbed against rawhide. But his mind raced with plans for escape. He knew that in a short time the Chogola would begin his long, slow execution.

And he knew they liked mutilating their enemies alive even more than after death!

BEST OF THE WEST
from Zebra Books

THOMPSON'S MOUNTAIN   (2042, $3.95)
by G. Clifton Wisler

Jeff Thompson was a boy of fifteen when his pa refused to sell out his mountain to the Union Pacific and got gunned down in return, along with the boy's mother. Jeff fled to Colorado, but he knew he'd even the score with the railroad man who had his parents killed . . . and either death or glory was at the end of the vengeance trail he'd blaze!

BROTHER WOLF   (1728, $2.95)
by Dan Parkinson

Only two men could help Lattimer run down the sheriff's killers—a stranger named Stillwell and an Apache who was as deadly with a Colt as he was with a knife. One of them would see justice done—from the muzzle of a six-gun.

BLOOD ARROW   (1549, $2.50)
by Dan Parkinson

Randall Kerry returned to his camp to find his companion slaughtered and scalped. With a war cry as wild as the savages,' the young scout raced forward with his pistol held high to meet them in battle.

THUNDERLAND   (1991, $3.50)
by Dan Parkinson

Men were suddenly dying all around Jonathan, and he needed to know why—before he became the next bloody victim of the ancient sword that would shape the future of the Texas frontier.

Available wherever paperbacks are sold, or order direct from the Publisher. Send cover price plus 50¢ per copy for mailing and handling to Zebra Books, Dept. 2436, 475 Park Avenue South, New York, N.Y. 10016. Residents of New York, New Jersey and Pennsylvania must include sales tax. DO NOT SEND CASH.

SABERS WEST

Patrick E. Andrews

ZEBRA BOOKS
KENSINGTON PUBLISHING CORP.

ZEBRA BOOKS

are published by

Kensington Publishing Corp.
475 Park Avenue South
New York, NY 10016

First printing: August, 1988

Printed in the United States of America

This Book is Dedicated to

Army Blue

HISTORICAL NOTE

Regiments and squadrons of the old horse cavalry and modern armored cavalry are made up of "troops." However, in this novel the term "company" is used to keep the story within the proper historical perspective. This was the official term used for these sub-units until 1883.

CHAPTER 1

Breezes gusted across the Red River and over the dark prairie before wafting through Fort Alexander's cantonment area. The spring sky stretched widely from far horizon to far horizon. Its inky blackness and glittering stars were unobstructed by even the slightest rise of ground from the table-flat terrain.

The dull glow of dozens of lanterns shone from the windows of the buildings around the post. This quartermaster-issued illumination lighted up the activities of the bored soldiery quartered in this small tract of civilization set down in the trackless wilderness. Most of the goings-on would be card games or masculine conversations filled with the lying boasts of young males. Most of these braggadocios were far from the homes they'd left after signing up for five-year hitches in the regular army.

But no matter what the men did to pass the empty hours of evening, alcohol would play a big part in fighting the grinding boredom. From the barracks to the sutler's store and even in the officers' quarters, soldiers whose brains had been dulled by monotonous and repetitious drill schedules were now comforted in clouds of quiet drunkenness.

On the north side of the garrison, the duty bugler stepped out of the guardhouse. He marched across the regimental parade ground to the flag pole standing tall in the center of the fort. He was a young Italian immigrant who found the flat plains country a stark contrast to the Alps of his native land. Trumpeter Benito Pullini might still be with his uncle in New York City if the old man hadn't insisted the youth stick with the long hours in his dark, dismal cobbler shop. Benito hadn't come all the way to America for that sort of life. Unable to speak much English at the time, Benito's only avenue of escape had been the army.

Benito put the bugle to his lips and blew *Call to Quarters,* the signal for all members of the garrison not on official duty to retire to their billets. The notes of the short air caused a flurry of activity around the fort. Non-commissioned officers, as drunk as their charges, who had been detailed to bedding down the lower-ranking enlisted men, began the task with expletive-sprinkled shouts. Those sergeants and corporals, with all the impatience of harried mothers putting their restless children to bed for the night, wanted to finish the job as quickly as possible.

The bugler sounded the call twice, each time to opposite sides of the garrison in the time-honored tradition. When the last note sounded, he marched back to the guardhouse with the same precision he'd demonstrated in going out to tend to the martial chore. He went inside the guard room and announced to the non-commissioned officer in charge, "Sergeant, I sound the *Call to Quarters."*

Sgt. Guy DuBose, reading a newspaper, looked up from where he sat with his booted feet propped up on the scarred table used by the N.C.O.s of the guard. "Yeah, Pullini," he remarked in a soft southern accent. "I heard you."

DuBose, with coal-black hair and moustache was a tall man whose slimness was that of hard muscularity. His natural handsomeness, made more rugged by the hard outdoor life he led, gave him an appearance that was much admired by the lower-ranking, younger soldiers. Many of them imitated him as best they could, sporting rather poorly nourished moustaches of their own while effecting the sergeant's preference for a red bandanna around the neck and a wide-brimmed hat for field duty.

The bugler, speaking more to practice English than out of necessity, nodded. "In fifteen minutes I got to sound the *Taps."*

"Right, Pullini," Guy DuBose, who had returned his full attention back to the periodical, answered without really hearing. He was deeply engrossed in a copy of the *New York Herald,* fresh after only five months of being passed from army post to army post starting at Jefferson Barracks, Missouri. It had wended its way via dispatches, transferred officers, and military transport, until finally arriving at headquarters of Fort Alexander, Texas. DuBose was reading about the re-election of U.S. Grant to the presidency despite the spate of scandals associated with his administration when a plaintive call sounded from the garrison yard.

"Corp'ral of the Guard, Post Number Two!"

DuBose looked across his newspaper at the cor-

11

poral, a big middle-aged Dane with a crooked nose. The Dane, named Hansen, stared back dully.

"Corp'ral of the Guard! Post Number Two!" the call was repeated. This time there was a note of urgency in the sentry's voice.

DuBose carefully folded the newspaper. "That'll be the sutler's store."

"*Ja,* and we know what that means," Hansen said. "Donovan."

"It wouldn't be anyone else," DuBose said. "You'll need help."

Hansen took his kepi and set it on his head in the regulation manner. "I would appreciate it, Sergeant."

DuBose got his own headgear and motioned the other N.C.O. to follow him. They walked out into the garrison and strode rapidly past Guard Post One. The soldier standing there grinned at them. "Sounds like Donovan's on a tear."

"Make a joke out of it," DuBose warned coldly, "and I'll drag you over there with us."

The youngster's expression faded to one of concern. "Right, Sergeant."

When the duo arrived at the sutler's store, they found the sentry at the bottom of the steps leading up to the frame building's porch. "Donovan's in there, Sergeant," the soldier reported. "He won't come out." He swallowed nervously. "I went in there like I was supposed to, and I said, 'Ever'body report to their barracks 'cause *Call to Quarters* is sounded.' I said that to 'em, Sergeant. Them's the exact words in the daily orders, ain't they?"

DuBose nodded. "What's your name, Trooper?"

"Horn," the youngster, all of eighteen, answered.

12

"Private Horn from 'C' Comp'ny, Sergeant."

"Very well, Private Horn. Is there anybody else in there with Donovan?" DuBose asked.

"Yes, Sergeant," Horn answered. "The sutler." ·

"Fine. Now you and the corporal follow me inside," DuBose said. "If we're lucky, Donovan will decide to leave peacefully."

Hansen spat. "Like hell he will!"

DuBose went up the steps with his two subordinates closely following. He went inside the store and made a quick survey of the situation.

A large balding Irishman, sporting a crooked nose that had been repeatedly broken in countless barracks room brawls, stood swaying at the bar. He held a tin cup in his hands. From all appearances, he had been about to take a drink from it when DuBose stepped into the room.

"Well, now," Donovan said. "If it ain't me own darlin' sargint come to see me." He quickly downed the whiskey and shoved the container at the sutler on the other side of the bar. "Another, Mister Dawkins!" The Irishman looked at DuBose. "Have ye come to down a few wit' me then, Sargint DuBose?"

"I have not," DuBose said sternly.

Donovan smiled and waved a finger at the sutler. "I'll be the only one to serve, Mister Dawkins."

The civilian sutler, holding a clay bottle, dutifully poured the liquor as ordered. But he spoke to DuBose. "I tried to get him to leave, Sergeant DuBose. But he wouldn't go."

"Aw, ye're a bluddy cry baby!" Donovan said grabbing the bottle. He took a few swigs directly from it. "Ah! Sure and that's the sweetest taste in God's

13

world—whiskey."

DuBose retained a passive expression. "Did you hear *Call to Quarters,* Donovan?"

"I did."

"Then I'm ordering you to obey it now," DuBose said.

"Y'know, Sargint, I have a lotta trouble with the daily service," Donovan said thickly. "Particular *Reveille* and *Call to Quarters.* I don't hear nothin' in the right ear, and only what I want in the left." He wiped his mouth with one huge mitt of a hand. "Now we're wasting time, bucko!" He swung the clay bottle around his head once, then threw it with all his strength straight at DuBose.

DuBose ducked, charging under the projectile, as he launched himself at Donovan. He could hear the bottle break against the far wall as he swung a roundhouse punch at Donovan's jaw.

The Irishman, despite his intoxication, nimbly ducked the blow, and punched straight out with his left, catching DuBose in the side of the head. DuBose staggered sideways, giving Corporal Hansen room to spring his own attack. Donovan was also ready for this, but Hansen was more the wrestler than the boxer and he grabbed the drunk around the waist, picking him up and slamming him hard against the bar. They bounced off, both losing their balance and crashing to the floor.

DuBose recovered enough from the hard jab to join in the pulling and rolling around on the floor. Donovan was enjoying himself to the hilt, laughing and hollering while freely bashing both his assailants.

"God damn it!" DuBose bellowed at the young sentry who stood petrified watching the brawl. "Give us a hand!"

Horn hesitated before reluctantly walking over to the struggling trio. He wet his lips and waited for the right opportunity. When it came, he raised his Springfield rifle in the proper butt-stroke position.

Then he struck.

The rifle butt slammed down hard onto Donovan's skull, making a sound like a sledge hammer hitting a rock. The Irishman's eyes rolled around twice, then he relaxed.

DuBose and Hansen struggled to their feet and looked down at the now peaceful man who had gone into a deep snooze. A large knot grew perceptively on his forehead.

The young soldier again licked his lips. "You won't tell him I was the one that done it, will you?"

"Give us a hand," DuBose ordered ignoring the fearful request.

Dawkins the sutler came around the bar. "Is he all right?"

Corporal Hansen smirked. "What's the matter, Dawkins? Afraid you'll lose your best customer?"

"Say now," Dawkins protested, "he's a friend o' mine."

"Shut up, Dawkins," DuBose said. "Come on, you two. Let's take him over to sleep it off."

The three dragged and pulled the unconscious drunk out of the store and down the steps. It took them a full fifteen minutes to get him across the garrison and back to the guard house. When they arrived, a couple of the off-duty sentries waiting to go on post lent a hand. Donovan, now a garrison prisoner, was dumped into one of the two empty cells used for

15

the fort's malefactors.

DuBose, winded by all the effort, stood by and watched as the new corporal of the guard relieved Hansen. The fresh duty N.C.O. marched out to post his sentries. After a quarter of an hour, all of Hansen's men were back in the guardhouse and settled down in their blankets spread along the floor to sleep away the next four hours before they again had to go out on post.

DuBose went back to his table and chair, picking up the newspaper he'd been taken from. He tried to read but couldn't maintain any interest in the news. After several attempts to read an article about the Three Emperors' League being established between Germany, Russia, and Austria-Hungary, he gave it up and stepped outside to enjoy a cigar in the cool night air.

Guy DuBose smoked languidly, enjoying the semi-solitude of standing in the dark. He gazed at this military post, an isolated part of an army where he had decided to spend the rest of his life.

It was called the United States Army, but it was more of a foreign legion. An overwhelming number of its soldiers were foreign-born. The majority used soldiering skills picked up as conscripts in Europe while they learned English—the first step in reaping the good life they sought in the New World. Others, mostly the native-born, were ne'er-do-wells, criminals, or naive young lads looking for adventure. They were ill-fed, poorly paid, badly used, brutally disciplined, unappreciated, and looked down on by the society they served.

To his former friends, the army would have seemed the last place they would find Guy DuBose. What would have shocked them more would be to know that he was serving as an enlisted man. Well-bred and educated, he seemed to possess all the qualities lacking in his barracks mates.

It would have seemed more appropriate for him to spend that particular evening in an elegant drawing room enjoying expensive cigars and brandy in the company of other gentlemen.

But the circumstances of his life had driven DuBose to enlist. He didn't go into the army seeking military glory. Instead, he pursued the anonymity and isolation such service offered.

DuBose continued to smoke, looking out past the buildings on the edge of the post. The country out there, still and serene under the prairie moon, eased from spring toward summer, but the warmer weather meant more than blooming flowers, abundant wildlife, and the sweet smell of buffalo grass. It was also the time of rolling violence, when the Indian warriors left their lodges to pursue their primary vocation: war.

CHAPTER 2

Guy Eduard DuBose had been born thirty-two years before in the year 1840. His entry into the mortal world, with the proverbial silver spoon firmly planted in his mouth, occurred in the city of Charleston, South Carolina. There, in that southern port city, his family ran a most prosperous export and import trade business.

His mother and father, although from diverse backgrounds, were a devoted couple who loved each other deeply. Their family origins, however, were widely separated in politics, philosophy and geographical location. The sire, Pierre Philippe DuBose, was descended from Huguenot settlers who had come to the colonies from France. He inherited the highly profitable commercial enterprise that operated in the port of Charleston and met his future wife, Prunella Platte, during a business trip to Boston. The young woman's people were staunch abolitionists, and their attitude toward this rather brash young southerner from a slave state could only be described as remote and reserved.

Pierre's saving grace, however, was the fact that neither he nor any of his relatives actually participated in that "peculiar institution"—as slavery was referred to in those days—due to the fact that they were all city businessmen without need of field hands or laborers. The DuBose house servants, as luck would have it for young Pierre, were either white or free black people.

When he was first introduced to Miss Platte at a Sunday outing with business acquaintances in Boston, the South Carolinian was not favorably impressed with the young woman despite her natural prettiness. To this dashing and flamboyant French-American, Prunella Platte seemed as cold as the cod pulled from her native Massachusetts waters. Unemotional and aloof, she seemed an undesirable opposite of the sassy, flirtatious belles of his home state.

But during other business trips and exposure to her company, he found a lighter side to the young woman, and he began an earnest courtship that eventually culminated in their marriage. The new Mrs. DuBose moved easily into southern society, keeping her opinions on slavery to herself, and only the closest and dearest of women friends knew of her Yankee attitudes.

Their only child, Guy Eduard, was born a year after the nuptials. The boy was pampered and catered to as was the custom of the times, until it was decided his training for manhood was to begin at about the age of twelve.

From that point on, the manly arts of riding, hunting, shooting, fencing and other pastimes of a young southern gentlemen were made a serious part of his upbringing. This was all done on the country estates of friends and relatives, where he learned to love the outdoor world and the adventures to be found there.

When Guy reached his late teens, his schooling was dedicated to business. This was not the hardheaded, frugal style of his mother's New England clan, but rather the honor system of handshakes and gentlemen's agreements preferred by the aristocrats of the South.

If there were any intellectual gaps in this education, his mother filled them by exposing her boy to the best in literature, music and the arts as she had learned them in the young ladies' finishing schools up north. Her efforts were certainly not wasted on the intelligent young man. Guy learned to appreciate these finer things which softened the edge of the other more martial and masculine lessons.

The social life of Charleston offered much for young Guy DuBose as he eased into his twenties. The city's elite held numerous balls and functions which drew their young people together in the proper, acceptable manner of the times. The belles were indulged, flattered, and feted by the young men who were taught to regard them as no less than the most sacred examples of womanhood.

But not so the women of the brothels.

The young men out on the plantations may have had the slave women to prey upon, but their counterparts in town indulged their basest passions with the harlots produced by a society in which the impoverished made up a substantial number. An evening spent catering to young ladies' whims and moods at a high-society ball would nearly always end with an after-party drunken gala in one of the numerous more expensive whore-houses Charleston had to offer.

Guy's passionate nature came more from his father's wilder side of the family than his mother's puritan forbearers. As randy as a rutting boar, he had been more than capable of getting his money's worth during a raid on a bordello, but eventually something happened that cooled this reckless lust.

He met a young lady named Pauline Berger.

She had moved to Charleston to stay in the home of an aunt and uncle. Their son and daughter, Selby and Glenna Berger, were contemporaries of Guy's, so it was only inevitable that he eventually be introduced to her. Pauline's loveliness also made it inevitable that Guy would fall deeply in love with the young woman. Willowy, with chestnut hair and bright blue eyes, she moved with a dancer's grace. Her face, with the small nose and arched eyebrows inherited from the European nobility in her bloodline, was lightly sprinkled with freckles that added to her feminine charm.

The first night after meeting her, Guy lay wakeful through the dark hours, her beautiful countenance dancing through his mind. For the first time in twenty years of life, he felt the sweet pain of infatuation. A party at her aunt and uncle's had been planned for the following Saturday night, and for the entire week preceding, Guy could think of nothing but Pauline Berger.

The social affair was one of the most emotionally painful of Guy's entire life. He found he was not the only one struck by the young lady's charms, and he was hard pressed to get more than a dance or two with her. Any conversation, without another hopeful swain standing nearby, was impossible.

From that night on, Guy forgot the bordellos. His affection grew from a boyish crush to mature love, and he decided to make his move. Lucky for him, Pauline's cousins Selby and Glenna had grown up with the hopeful suitor and preferred him above all others if Pauline was to have a sweetheart. With their help in arranging meetings that seemed only chance, putting in plenty of good words about him and his family, and seeing that any circumstances for getting close to her at parties were definitely in Guy's favor, the lover was ready to make his move.

The expression of love was made on the veranda on a hot summer day. All four of the young people had been enjoying lemonade and cookies while indulging in lighthearted conversation and jokes cracked by Guy and Selby. Glenna helped out as best she could by gushing over everything that Guy said in an attempt to put him in the best light possible. Finally, on a ruse that they had to tend to a matter with their mother, Selby and Glenna withdrew, leaving Guy to state his case.

He managed a weak smile at her, but looked away. Then he swallowed hard, and swiveled in his chair toward her. "Miss Pauline—"

"Yes, Mister DuBose?" Pauline displayed an innocent and unknowing expression although Glenna had long before told her of Guy's feelings toward her.

"I wonder, Miss Pauline," Guy said after preparing himself once again, "if I—"

"Yes, Mister DuBose?"

He took a deep breath and rattled off, "If I might come calling on you here." Guy paused again. "What I mean is that I would be most pleased if you would

23

allow me to be a caller."

Pauline feigned surprise. "Why, Mister DuBose! Am I to believe that you are asking to be my beau?"

Bringing it all out into the open gave him courage. "Yes, Miss Pauline. I would like very much to be your beau." He cleared his throat. "If I may."

"Well—" She seemed hesitant. "You are a very nice young man and I am most flattered, sir."

It seemed the preamble of a refusal, and his heart broke.

Then she said, "Thank you, Mister DuBose. I would be most happy to accept you as my beau."

Thus the romance began and flourished. One of the biggest obstacles was Guy's own parents. Pauline Berger, while quite respectable, was from an impoverished branch of the Berger family. She was an only child, and her parents had died in a typhoid epidemic in southern Georgia leaving her with nothing. She was, in truth, living on the charity of the other branch of the Berger family. Because of this genteel but very real poverty, there would be no dowry, no business connections, and no social advantages whatsoever to a marriage with her, but Pauline's comeliness and appeal were such that Mr. and Mrs. DuBose eventually accepted her as their future daughter-in-law.

Although Guy's life was, for the most part, consumed with his overwhelming affections for Pauline, he managed to find time for other interests as well. Besides the excitement and demands of going into the family business—his formal schooling had ended in his eighteenth year—he was a member of a fancy militia regiment called the Charleston Zouaves.

Although a legal organization within the state's military system, the Zouaves were actually an exclusive men's club. These wealthy citizen-soldiers paid a former regular army sergeant to act as their drill instructor, so that their marching and other activities on muster days would be correct and proper.

The regiment's uniforms, paid for by the members themselves, were modeled somewhat after the Algerian Zouaves of the French colonial army. They wore red kepis with gold trimming, short gray jackets also faced with gold, and baggy red trousers stuffed into white leggings. Wide sashes and shiny black leather accouterments completed the effect.

Once a month these stalwarts would don their fancy uniforms and meet at Pinckney Square to go through a couple of hours of drilling before an indulgent audience made up of gushing wives, admiring sweethearts, and thoroughly amused male friends. Guy, who served as a corporal, liked the opportunity to dress up and show off in front of Pauline. She responded with the proper adoration and praise as Guy strutted about with his musket and bayonet, wheeling and turning to the shouted orders of their colonel—who was carefully and subtly coached by the ex-sergeant.

It all had a sort of comic opera look about it until Fort Sumter was fired on April 12, 1861 by batteries in Charleston's Harbor.

The Zouaves, not being artillerists, were merely spectators to the bombardment, but their own participation in the war began the next day when they were mustered into Confederate service and sent north to begin their participation in the most vicious war America was to ever fight.

Guy's farewell to Pauline was touching. The two, enormously saddened by this separation and delay in their marriage plans, swore eternal love and devotion to one another. They parted reluctantly and sadly at the railroad station as the regiment boarded the train to take them to whatever glory the war held in store for it.

The Zouaves traveled through North Carolina and up to Virginia to join General Robert E. Lee and begin a bloody odyssey. The initial concept of a war that would be won quickly and gloriously faded fast on the road that took them through such man-made hells as Bull Run, Shiloh, Antietam, and Gettysburg.

The Zouaves' regiment changed much during that time. Their fancy uniforms, more suitable for parading than fighting, soon grew tattered and were replaced by plainer military clothing until even those stocks ran out. As the Confederacy's war treasury was drained, the Zouaves suffered along with the rest of the southern army. Within a couple of years they were reduced to eating parched corn and looting shoes off Yankee corpses while wearing cheap, tattered butternut uniforms. This inglorious, humble color was made necessary by the Federal sea blockade which kept the ingredients for proper dyes and coloring from coming into Confederate port cities.

Guy DuBose suffered with the rest, but he comforted himself by reading and rereading the letters he received from Pauline. Somehow, knowing that her love was true and that she waited for him, gave him the moral support and optimism he needed to endure the terrible experiences of bloody skirmishes and thundering battles.

He went from a naive corporal to a hardened

26

captain, his outfit dwindled in numbers while sustaining horrible casualty rates in the bloody fighting. By the time the Battle of Gettysburg had begun, the Charleston Zouaves was a regiment in name only. On the third morning of the fighting, when they were attached to General George Pickett's Virginia troops for the last desperate charge to save the battle, the formerly fancy militia unit could muster no more than sixty ragged soldiers.

That final effort began when the Confederate ranks, properly dressed and covered down, advanced into the overwhelming musketry and cannonade of the blue-clad Yankee until, finally, bodies and hearts broken, their assault failed. When the remnants of the Johnny Rebs withdrew from the horrible field, Capt. Guy DuBose was left behind badly wounded.

He spent the remaining two years of the war in a Federal prison camp in Illinois, completely cut off from home. He could have received a parole if he'd signed a statement of loyalty to the United States government and promise never again to raise arms against the United States of America. Guy, a proud South Carolinian, refused. This stubbornness damned him to an unspeakable imprisonment. He suffered from bad weather, cruel treatment, and near starvation. But he persevered, as always, strengthened by the love of Pauline Berger. Although unable to correspond with his sweetheart, he strongly sensed her presence from ceaselessly thinking of her. During the most miserable hours of his captivity, he found strength in knowing that she waited for him at the end of the long, forlorn road of war.

The young officer's conduct in Yankee hands would

have been entirely different if he'd known one startling fact: a friend who had seen him fall at Gettysburg had erroneously informed his family and Pauline Berger that he had been killed in the battle. Everyone he knew in Charleston thought him dead.

The war came to a close when Gen. Robert E. Lee of the Confederacy and Gen. Ulysses S. Grant of the Federals signed the formal surrender at Appomattox. The rebel prisoners in the camp were marched to the nearest railroad and put aboard southern-bound trains. They traveled for four days before finally reaching Virginia where they were left to find their own way back to their various homes.

Ex-Captain Guy DuBose walked the entire distance to Charleston. When he finally arrived after more than a month on the road, he found his home very much changed. The years of conflict had been harsh. His family's import business had failed, but the worst, most unbelievable news he received upon his return was that Pauline—his own beloved Pauline—had married an officer in the occupying Union forces policing Charleston. She had already gone north with her new husband by the time Guy returned to Charleston.

He spent almost an entire year trying to adjust to a postwar situation that he found intolerable. Broken-hearted and bitter, he could not make any of the plans affecting his personal and business life come to success. Drinking heavily and failing morally and physically, his former friends turned away from him as they devoted their energies and hopes into rebuilding their own broken lives.

Finally, in the drab January of 1867, Guy realized there was only one profession that he knew well. The years of fighting had taught him a violent skill, but at least it was one that would put food in his stomach and take him away from the shame of failure.

He enlisted in the army and donned the same blue uniform that he had spent four years fighting.

Pvt. Guy DuBose was sent to a frontier cavalry regiment where he found a strange satisfaction. Although his service in the Confederacy precluded any chance of becoming an officer, Guy found in that monastic life what he really needed: forgetfulness.

He wanted to forget the past, the useless sacrifices and suffering in the war, and, most of all he craved to forget Pauline Berger. Cut off from a society he could not tolerate, the ex-Confederate found the rough-and-tumble barracks life completely to his liking. Guy's superiors recognized his talents. A natural soldier and leader, he was promoted to corporal after a year's service. Two more years after that, he was awarded a sergeancy.

The only bitterness he felt emerged periodically in spasms of heavy, almost desperate drinking when the memory of the woman he still loved would leap unbidden into his conscious mind. Only the numbing effects of strong, unwatered whiskey would drive the heartbreak away.

CHAPTER 3

The entire regiment was drawn up for Fort Alexander's regular Sunday dismounted parade. The spectators of this ceremony were few, mostly wives and children who viewed any change in the dreary schedule of weekdays as something to watch. There were also a few Indians from the nearby Red River Agency, who watched out of curiosity at what they presumed was some sort of religious or medicine-making ceremony of the white men.

The garrison's troops stood in an unmoving formation, adorned in their full-dress uniforms. A glance across their ranks showed the Black Prussian-style helmets with yellow horsetail plumes streaming down the back, dominating this scene of gold and blue splashed across the small area set in the middle of the wilderness.

The rest of this fancy martial attire consisted of high-collared blue tunics with yellow facings, epaulets and chevrons. Light blue trousers, with yellow stripes for the officers and N.C.O.s, were worn outside the boots rather than stuffed into them for this most formal of military occasions. The higher-ranking members of the regiment carried sabers while the corporals and privates sported U.S. model 1870 Springfield carbines. It was a striking sight. Even the most ardent grumblers among the enlisted men kept their shoulders square and marched with precision knowing they created a handsome martial display.

There were audible snaps of hands slapping leather slings, and the sharp crack of heels as the troops wheeled from column to flank formations. Sharp, abrupt shouts of command from N.C.O.s and officers took them through the well-drilled movements that brought them into their proper places in the regimental parade.

This was the regular army, disciplined and professional, going through their fanciest martial paces.

Rather than have a single trumpeter sound the signal, the entire regimental band struck up *Adjutant's Call*. The adjutant, a harried first lieutenant named Harris, marched up to the head of the formation where the colonel commanding the regiment stood. After properly reporting, Lieutenant Harris went to his post.

That was the signal for the band to launch into the regimental song *When Johnny Comes Marching Home Again*. This air from the war was a favorite of the colonel's and chosen by him to be their official march. While the music played, the three squadrons passed in review, then wheeled about to return to their original positions.

Once again the adjutant made an appearance, saluting the colonel. After the proper exchange of words in the ritual, the commander left the field, and the adjutant made an about-face. The squadrons were given over to the majors who gave them over to the company commanders. They, in turn, relinquished their commands to the first sergeants who marched the men back to their barracks and dismissed them. By that time the officers had drifted back to their quarters.

The men went inside their barracks and deposited their weapons in the racks and waited for the sounding of *Church Call*. Every man answered the summons and fell into formation to march to the post chapel to hear the chaplain's sermon for that particular Sunday. This was not because of any deep-seated religious fervor or devotion on their part. Any able-bodied soldier not attending services would find himself pulling unpleasant fatigue duties under the stern supervision of the regimental sergeant major. By going to chapel, they knew they would be free afterward to change back into regular uniform and while away the rest of Sunday in relative freedom.

Sgt. Guy DuBose was among those participating in this weekly practice. Uncomfortable in the restraining collar, he sat on the hard wooden bench that served as a pew in the non-commissioned officers' section of the chapel. A few wives and wiggling children belonging to the professional soldiers were spread out among the blue uniforms. To the front were the officers with their families while the rear of the small church was occupied by the privates—all bachelors—who squirmed with the same impatience demonstrated by the kids.

The chaplain, a thin, hawkish man in his middle age, was inconsiderate of his captive audience. He droned through a dull, pointless sermon, the monotone of his voice lulling several troopers to sleep. However, for decorum's sake, several corporals who were stationed in strategic places just for such an event gave the nodding offenders a subtle, but sharp punch in the ribs.

But eventually the final benediction was pronounced, and the chaplain left his pulpit to walk down the aisle and lead his congregation to the outside world and freedom.

The officers and their ladies exited first, making hasty goodbys before going back to their quarters to spend quiet Sunday afternoons visiting each other. Several, because of the good weather and the lack of hostile Indian activity, had planned picnics. Back in a half dozen of the sod and frame homes, cold fried chicken and baked goodies nestled in baskets on kitchen tables, waiting to be taken out into the countryside.

Guy DuBose walked outside with the other sergeants, but instead of falling in with his fellow N.C.O.s he split off by himself and hurried back to the barracks. He wasted no time in going to his bunk in an area partitioned off from the rest of the squad room. As a non-commissioned officer, this semi-privacy was a privilege accorded him per regulations.

He quickly shucked himself out of the constraints of full dress and climbed into the more comfortable sack coat and trousers of the regular uniform. After seeing that his fancier clothing was properly hung up to avoid wrinkles, he went to the wooden locker box sitting in its prescribed place at the foot of his bunk. He pulled the issue .44 caliber Remington revolver from its place in the top tray. After inserting the loaded cylinder into the pistol, he put the weapon in his haversack and slung it over his shoulder. Next, Guy donned his kepi and

34

picked up his laundry bag, ready to leave.

By the time he walked back through the barracks, the other troopers were also changing. He walked without speaking down the aisle between their bunks and stepped outside.

Pvt. Tim Donovan, released earlier that same morning after serving his time in the guardhouse, stood outside the barracks. The big Irishman had a mournful expression on his brutal face. He raised a finger tip to the brim of his kepi. "Now then, the top o' the mornin' to ye, Sargint DuBose."

"How're you doing, Donovan?" Guy asked. Three days previously, the first morning after the brawl at the sutler's store, Donovan had been bucked and gagged. That meant his wrists had been bound to his ankles, and a stick, held in place by a cruelly knotted bandanna, was in his mouth. When Guy had seen him later the same day, the man had been lying on his side unconscious with his eyes wide open. Only a liberal splashing of water from a lister bucket had brought him around.

Donovan shifted his feet and snuffed, looking down at the ground. "It's back to duty they've sent me, Sargint," he said. "And now that I've the chance, I'd like to apologize for me behavior over to the sutler's when you was the sargint o' the guard."

Guy grinned a little. The knot on Donovan's head where the young sentry had butt-stroked him had gone down, but there was still plenty of discoloration around his eyes. "I'd say you got the worst of it."

"And, sure, I deserved the worst, Sargint," Donovan said. "I swear I'm gonna jine up wit' the Good Templars." He referred to a small group of teetotalers in the regiment who had banded together under an oath of abstinence.

"Well," Guy drawled. "I'm not angry, Donovan. Let's let bygones be bygones. After all, you are in my section. I just want you to try to control yourself when you get drunk."

"I won't be gittin' drunk for awhile now," Donovan said. "They gimme a fine o' three month's pay on top o' that stint in the guardhouse." He shuffled his feet around. "Which brings to mind—" He let the words hang.

Guy smiled again, shaking his head. He reached into his pocket and pulled a dollar out. "Pay me back in three months then."

"Sure now, and ye're a good man, Sargint DuBose," Donovan said happily taking the money. "I'll foller you to hell itself, and if the devil gives you any trouble, why I'll put a .50 caliber ball in him meself from me own darlin' Springfield." He looked at the laundry bag that Guy carried. "Are ye off to Soap Suds Row then?" That was the section of the post where the married sergeants, whose wives worked as laundresses, were quartered.

"Right," Guy said. He patted the haversack. "Then a walk in the country."

"Do ye have a pistol in there?" Donovan inquired. "It's the time o' year the Injuns git restless, Sargint."

"I'm armed."

"Well, if ye'd prefer to start yer walk now, I'd be happy to take the laundry over fer ye," Donovan offered.

"I'll do it," Guy responded. "I could use a taste of Mrs. Tate's coffee." He nodded a goodby, and strode off.

Guy made a stop at the sutler's store first. He purchased two bottles of whiskey, and stuck them in the haversack with the pistol.

"Hey, DuBose!" McClary, the first sergeant of C Company, was sitting with two other non-coms. "Have a drink."

"No, thanks," Guy said. "I have some things to attend to."

One of the other sergeants leered. "The hog ranch won't be open for business 'til later, DuBose." He referred to the rustic bordello an enterprising whiskey dealer had set up at the edge of the military reservation.

Dawkins, the sutler, called over from his counter. "All you'll get over there is bad likker and the clap!" The hog ranch cut into his business. The opportunity to consort with easy women, even unattractive down-and-outers, lured his soldier-customers away. As a civilian contractor, he faced as much a chance of going broke as any businessman.

Guy grinned and waved at the other N.C.O.s as he left the store and turned south, walking through the Third Squadron's barracks over to Soap Suds Row. That area, made up of one single, neatly spaced line of sod houses, was a noisy, rollicking neighborhood. Countless children—army brats—scampered around yelling as loud as their small lungs would allow. Their parents, oblivious to the minor riot around them, relaxed outside their crude domiciles enjoying this first warmth after a particularly hard winter.

Guy wasted no time in going to the home of his friend Sgt. Harry Tate. Tate, a Georgian and also an ex-Confederate, served in "C" Company leading the Second Section. His entry into the army had been out

37

of the prison camp at Rock Island, Illinois. Once settled in, he'd saved his money for more than a year to send for his family.

Tate's wife Martha was a wide-hipped woman who had birthed fourteen children into the world. The harshness of her life, both in the hills of their native state and in the army, was evident in the fact that only three of them had survived their second year.

Harry, puffing on a corncob pipe, was seated on a three-legged stool at the door of his soddie. When he saw Guy approaching, he turned his head toward the door. "Marfy! Marfy! Hyeah comes ol' Guy."

Martha Tate appeared in the doorway. She waved at Guy, then scurried out to meet him. "How do, Mister DuBose." She always displayed an abundance of deference toward Guy. It wasn't contrived or hypocritical conduct on Martha's part. As a poor southerner, she'd been brought up to respect "better folks" who deserved such courtesy. Guy DuBose, despite his rank, was more of a gentleman to Martha Tate than even the colonel commanding.

Accordingly, Guy always went out of his way to be gracious and polite toward her. "Good morning, Mrs. Tate. I have brought you my weekly washing, if you please."

"O'course, Mister DuBose," Martha said, taking the bag. Like the other laundresses, she received two dollars a month from each customer to wash and iron their clothing. "Will you take a cup o' cawfee?" Martha asked.

"I'd be most pleased," Guy said.

Martha went inside and reappeared with a stool similar to the one her husband Harry was seated on.

"Now sit yorese'f down. I won't be a minute."

"I'll take a cup too," Harry announced. "Go on like Marfy said and sit down, Guy." He looked up at the sun radiating down over the countryside. "Gonna take yore walk, are ya?" He referred to the habit that Guy had developed some time previously.

"Yes," Guy answered. "The weather has warmed up nicely." He removed his haversack after pulling a bottle of the whiskey from it.

"It shore has," Harry answered hungrily eyeing the liquor now sitting between them. Supporting even a small family on army pay and the extra laundry money didn't give him the opportunity to drink as abundantly as he would have preferred.

Martha came out with two tin cups of steaming coffee. She served the men, then disappeared back into the house to tend to her late Sunday morning chores.

Guy, without waiting, poured a generous drink into Harry's cup. The two sipped the hot brew silently for a few moments.

Harry held his cup between his hands. "I wonder when the new cap'n is gonna git here."

Guy shrugged. "It's hard to tell. He's long overdue." He took a sip of the coffee, savoring the whiskey in it. "But there is nothing unusual in that."

Harry laughed. "He musta really ruffled some perty fancy feathers, whoever he is."

"Indeed," Guy agreed. "An officer doesn't get transferred from the Adjutant General's Department in Washington City out to this godforsaken place without having committed some unforgivable *faux pas.*"

"How's that?" Harry asked.

"He made the wrong fellow mad at him," Guy explained.

"Well, he's a brevet lieutenant colonel," Harry said, "for whatever that's worth." He laughed again, and lowered his voice. "Them damn Yankees got more damn brevet ranks than a Georgia hound's got fleas."

"I'm sure we'll get the full story when he gets out here and the sergeant major can see his records," Guy said. He quickly finished off the coffee and stood up. "Thank you for the coffee, Mrs. Tate," he said loudly.

Martha came back outside. "Would you care fer more, Mister DuBose?"

"No, thank you kindly," Guy said. "It was delicious, but I'm anxious to take a walk. It's been a long winter."

Martha took the cup. "It was nice to have you visit, Mister DuBose. You have a nice walk now, heah?"

"Thank you," Guy said. He nodded to Harry. "See you tomorrow morning."

"At reveille," Harry replied. "Standing tall and sharp in Yankee blue, boy!"

Guy laughed at the other's barbed humor. He walked out of Soap Suds Row and headed for the open country on the other side of the creek where the N.C.O.s' wives tended to their laundry chores.

He strode along briskly for twenty minutes, his destination barely visible over the horizon. It was a cottonwood tree growing on the bank of the same creek that wound and snaked its way through the tall prairie grass to flow into Fort Alexander.

When Guy arrived, he sat down and pulled the whiskey from the haversack. After arranging the canvas carrier so that he would be able to get to the pistol quickly if necessary, he treated himself to the

40

first, throat-searing swallow of liquor.

The alcohol warmed his stomach, but it took several more quick gulps of the stuff before the buzz began in his mind. The painful memory of Pauline—beautiful, treacherous, faithless Pauline—had been gnawing at him every waking moment for the previous several days. When she'd begun to invade his dreams, Guy knew it was time for a good, deep solitary drunk.

He drank again, the hum of the liquor's effect dulling the pain in his heart. Guy fully realized it was only temporary relief, but at least it was an emotional balm of sorts that gave him a period of bearable peace.

Guy's only contact with women had been occasional bouts with frontier prostitutes. Even a broken-hearted male had physical needs, but he had to be heavily intoxicated and completely uninhibited before he could seek even that physical release.

He settled into slow steady drinking, growing melancholy and drunk. His vision blurred a bit as he finished off the first bottle. He opened the second and raised it in a toast. "Here's to life now," he said in a whisper to himself. "And to what might have been, but will never be."

He smiled sardonically, thinking of the similarity in his sad existence between the army and the whiskey he consumed: each closed out unpleasant realities and took him farther and farther from an existence that had ended over ten years ago.

The sun rolled slowly across the sky, finally dipping toward the western horizon, while the sad professional soldier sank deeper into the blissful forgetfulness of profound intoxication.

CHAPTER 4

The spring season that had eased away the cruel winter heralded more than a change in the weather for Fort Alexander. Besides making life much more pleasant it was a time for the quarterly beef issue to the Indians staying on the reservation at the Red River Agency. This task was handled by the army through civilian beef contractors who had made successful bids with the government.

The tribe confined by treaty to that area was the Chogola Comanches, an offshoot of the larger clan. They were led, as far as the whites were concerned, by an old chief named Talks-To-Them. This perception of leadership, however, was not totally shared by the Chogolas themselves. These independently-minded aborigines recognized no permanent seat of leadership in their culture. If a certain individual happened to be popular and prove himself wise, he might enjoy a brief stint at the helm of the tribal council, but that was all. War parties were generally formed up by several warriors in a haphazard fashion with a common goal stated before they left camp.

The Chogolas, furthermore, were split into several factions. The most vociferous was a warrior society called the Hawks-of-the-Wind, who displayed a disturbing tendency to pay heed to a particularly ferocious individual named Lame Elk.

Lame Elk was openly contemptuous of Talks-To-Them, insulting the old man at every opportunity. But Lame Elk's main problem with the tribal elder was the fact that Talks-To-Them's years of experience—particularly with white men—had given him a sort of political savvy and intuitive judgement which led him to numerous correct choices when it came to dealing with the complex invaders of their lands.

In fact, it was because of Talks-To-Them's counsel that the tribe had settled on the Red River Agency. In exchange for this, they received four issues of government beef a year and agreed to have the adult men learn farming while all the children went to school to be educated in the white man's way.

The U.S. government's basic aim in this, of course, was to turn the Chogolas from the Indian way to that of the civilized world, not so much to benefit the Chogolas but to bring them under the influence and authority of the army. The government hoped to curb their natural warlike tendencies so that the settlement of Texas and Kansas could continue without the constant interruption of Indian warfare.

There was an exception to this hypothesis among the whites. Elements of caring people sincerely wanted the Indians to benefit from close contact with civilization. The Chogolas, during the previous years, had become the targets of a genuine and honest program to educate

44

and enlighten them.

This schooling was conducted under the kind supervision and administration of the government agent and his wife. The couple, members of the Christian Pacification Society, was Palmer and Netta Druce. Their parent organization had gained some political favor in Washington through contacts deep within the Bureau of Indian Affairs. Two members of the church—for that was what the society really was— were among the upper echelons of the bureau. Their influence brought about the appointment of several of their brethren to minister to the various tribes being brought under the control of the Federal Government.

All of this happened a great distance from Fort Alexander, but brought marked consequences not only to the post and the agency, but to the people of western Texas.

Now, at the Red River Agency, the Druces and Indians had risen early to prepare for the arrival of the government cattle issue. At the same time, Sgt. Guy DuBose had awakened from his lonely drunk. It was an hour before dawn. Nauseous, stiff and dampened by the early morning dew, he made his way back to the barracks to change into a fresh uniform. By the time *Reveille* was sounded, he had recovered fully, turning out his section with his friend Harry Tate, who awoke his own troopers with yells and the stomping of boots to accompany the noisy trumpeter.

Normal drill was suspended for Guy and his men that day. They were detailed to accompany the regimental quartermaster out to the agency that morning to oversee the issue of the government cattle to the Chogolas. The herd, brought in from the railhead at Dahlquart, was being held on the south post by a crew of drovers.

Guy marched his twenty soldiers over to the stables to saddle their mounts and prepare for the ride across the river to the agency. Pvt. Tim Donovan was among the group. He'd made good on his pledge of joining the Good Templars. After several days of strict sobriety, the ruddy puffiness in his face had subsided somewhat, and he'd taken on a healthier look.

It took but a brief fifteen minutes for the well-drilled troops to be fully prepared for the ride. When all were ready, they walked the horses over to the main gate to wait for the quartermaster.

The gate was not actually a set of portals since Fort Alexander was not a walled fort. It was simply the main entrance into the garrison, and a formal guard was always stationed there. Guy's men, anxious to get out of the area after weeks of being confined to the post, fidgeted until the quartermaster finally arrived. He was a seasoned officer, long past due for promotion, who served in the rank of first lieutenant. Named Robertson, he was hard-drinking and gruff. He wasted little time on ceremony. After returning Guy's salute, he gave the troops a quick glance of inspection. "Fine," he announced. "Now let's get this over with," he said. "I want the cattle issued to those Redskin bastards before the colonel shows up."

"The colonel?" Guy asked. "I didn't expect him out there today."

"Neither did I, Sergeant," Robertson said. "But evidently Mr. and Mrs. Druce are worried about Lame Elk. He's been a rather unpleasant fellow around the

46

agency lately. They feel he needs a talking to by our beloved regimental commander."

"That won't impress Lame Elk," Guy said.

"Perhaps not," Robertson replied. "But the Druces will feel better." He spat. "God damned Sunday school teachers trying to run an Indian agency!"

Guy turned to his section who stood in proper formation waiting for the day's work to begin. "Prepare to mount! Mount!" The men swung up into their saddles. Guy stepped into his own stirrup and settled in for the ride. "Fours right!" He shouted. "March!" They followed the officer and sergeant out through the main gate.

The small column turned north and cantered out over the flat prairie. Meadowlarks' calls were interrupted by the pounding of hooves. They crossed the Red River at a shallow place called Comanche Ford. Once they had reached the center of the water, they were no longer in Texas, but had crossed the invisible boundary into Indian Territory.

The Red River Agency was located a mile and a half from Fort Alexander. It consisted of several permanent buildings clustered close together serving as the residence, trading post and headquarters for the agent. A fluid, never permanent arrangement of lodges, which the Indians moved at their various whims, was scattered around this central area. Arguments, restlessness, and accumulating filth generated the continuing mobility.

Mr. and Mrs. Palmer Druce had heard the troopers approaching and were out in the yard when the blue-clad soldiers rode into the agency yard. Druce, as usual, was dressed somberly in a black suit. He touched

47

his hand to the brim of his wide, shallow-crowned hat and smiled a greeting. "Good morning to you, Mr. Robertson. And to you, Sergeant DuBose."

Netta Druce stood beside her husband. She displayed a slight smile, her eyes darting over toward Guy. The sergeant knew she found him attractive, and he also surmised that life with her husband must be quite tedious and dull a great deal of the time. In spite of her obvious bent toward religion, Guy had wondered if a casual, infrequent affair could be started up with her. This wasn't so much out of lust on his part as it was loneliness for feminine company. In fact, he would have been content with clandestine, quiet moments of conversation with her. It would have been a charming contrast to the usual coarse exchanges he had with his fellow soldiers.

Netta Druce was a short, plumpish young woman with a round, plain face. She wore her hair in a tight bun, and she moved about in a prim and proper manner. Guy had made a couple of friendly, innocent overtures toward her to test the waters for that special friendship he desired. But Mrs. Druce was decidedly shy and uneasy in his presence during those rare times he had the opportunity to speak to her. It became obvious after several more attempts at establishing some sort of rapport, that it would be impossible to arrange any rendezvous with her, no matter how innocent.

Guy turned his attention back to his troops. He ordered them to dismount, but to stand fast beside their horses. Several Chogola, knowing that it was beef-issue day, had begun to gather around.

Druce peered out into the prairie. "I see the cattle are

48

not with you."

"They will arrive within a couple of hours," Robertson explained. "I am also to inform you that Colonel Gatley will be here at noon."

"That is good to hear," Druce said. "I hate to sound a sour note, but I fear that Lame Elk has grown boastful and arrogant. A good talking to should settle him down."

Guy was interested. "Has he made any threats?"

"Not toward the agency itself, Sergeant DuBose," Druce answered. "But he has complained bitterly about the conditions here. I need not point out to you the evil that Indian can commit."

Guy, who had spent the entire summer a year before campaigning against the Indian war chief, was well aware of how far the man would go. Several troopers and Indians had died in the bloody conflicts before Lame Elk could be convinced it was to his benefit to return to the agency.

Even then, Guy knew that Lame Elk had agreed to the treaty-within-a-treaty only to be able to winter comfortably at the Red River Agency and draw some government beef. The Chogola was far from being an erratic hothead. His emotionally charged temperament was tempered by an ability to coldly calculate and estimate how far he could go and get away with it.

By the time the cattle herd arrived, every man, woman, and child of the Chogola Comanche tribe had gathered around the agency buildings. Many of the warriors were only contemptuous of the soldiers, sneering and leering at them. The troopers, on the other hand, gave back as much as they took. At one point, Guy had to keep a couple of his men from answering the silent taunts with shouts and insults.

The old chief Talks-To-Them did not deign to make an appearance until the cattle showed up. After the noisy arrival of the bawling herd driven by a crew of cowboys who looked as wild as the gathering Indians, Talks-To-Them made a silent appearance trailed by his two wives. He was a wizened elder, with deep wrinkles in his bronze face. His iron-gray braids hung down his back against his red flannel shirt. His bowed legs looked like copper saplings under the loincloth. Talks-To-Them looked over at DuBose. He nodded to the sergeant, and pointed over to the cattle. "You count them cows, Rides-All-Day?"

Guy shook his head. "I haven't had a chance." He had gotten the name Rides-All-Day from the tenacity he'd shown in tracking down warriors who left the agency.

"Look at those cows," Talks-To-Them scowled. "They look skinny without much meat."

Robertson interrupted. "Then fatten them on the grass around here. You don't have to butcher them the same day they're given to you."

"My people are hungry," Talks-To-Them said. "It has been a long winter. All the cows from three moons back long ago gone. And you won't let us hunt buffalo."

"You can hunt buffalo," Robertson countered. "Just don't do it down in Texas or in Kansas."

Talks-To-Them ignored the officer. Instead he spoke directly to DuBose. "The buffalo go where they must go as always. They don't care about treaties we make. The young men are angry, Rides-All-Day. Promises are not kept."

"The colonel is coming to see you," Guy said. "He will be here after the beef issue."

It was obvious that Talks-To-Them was going to play a game of wits. "He won't do no good. Young men are a lot angry, Rides-All-Day. It is hard for me to tell them what to do. They won't listen."

"Talk to the colonel," Guy said.

"Why we don't talk to you, Rides-All-Day? You are a smart man," Talks-To-Them said.

"I am not a chief," Guy explained.

Talks-To-Them pointed to the cavalry section. "You are the chief of those soldiers."

"That is not enough to make me a big chief," Guy said.

They were interrupted when the drovers' foreman left the herd under the care of his cowboys. He pulled some papers from the leather vest he wore. "Who signs for them cows?"

"I will," Robertson said. "How many are there?"

"It says on the paper two hunnerd head," the drover said.

DuBose glared at the man. "He didn't ask you what it said on the paper. He asked you how many are in the herd."

The man, a rough character in his own right, sized up the tall sergeant. He decided it wouldn't be a good idea to press the matter physically, but he nevertheless wasn't going to be pushed around. "Well, soljer boy, I'd say two-hunnerd."

Robertson scribbled his name, rank, and regiment across the receipt. "I've taken delivery."

"Then I'll bid y'all a good day," the man said. He looked at DuBose. "You can count 'em all you want now, soljer boy."

DuBose turned to the officer. "Sir, it's a certainty that the herd is short."

"I agree," Robertson said calmly. "But I'll be damned if I'll get involved in a drawn-out paperwork matter that will take a great deal of time."

"Sir—"

"Sergeant DuBose," Robertson said sharply. "As the regimental quartermaster I have enough to do in tending to the regular duties of my office. This extra work posed by administering to a bunch of Indians at an agency run by religious zealots is not welcomed nor does it earn my enthusiastic interest."

"Yes, sir," Guy said. "But when the meat runs out, the Indians are going to go back to hell raising. That gives Lame Elk the perfect excuse for breaking out of the reservation."

"Then, Sergeant," Robertson said wearily, "let's kill the son of a bitch and all the sons of bitches that follow him. That should solve *my* problems, *your* problems, and the *government's* problems."

"Yes, sir."

"By the way, the adjutant tells me your new company commander should be arriving next week."

"Yes, sir."

Robertson laughed. "I'm curious as hell to see whose toes he's been treading on. I understand he's a married man. I suspect his wife will find our Fort Alexander a real trial after living in luxury in Washington City."

"Yes, sir."

"Of course she can bring our wives up to date on the latest fashions," Robertson mused. "My old woman's wardrobe must be ten or fifteen years out of date."

"It will be an interesting affair for the officers' ladies," Guy agreed.

The Indians had turned their attention to the cattle. The warriors, now mounted, were rather inexpertly herding the cows away as if they were driving a herd of buffalo. Only a few of the warriors stayed. Among those was Lame Elk. He walked over to the far side of the agency with several of his followers, obviously snubbing Talks-To-Them and the soldiers.

The Indians knew that Colonel Gatley wanted to speak to them that morning. But his tardiness did not upset them. In their world only the seasons counted for the passage of time. The importance in this was not to keep track of the years necessarily; it was more for the planning of hunting and war, and choosing the most comfortable place to camp.

The soldiers also felt no impatience. The ride over to the agency had been a welcome break in the tedium of drill and fatigue duties. They were glad for even this short trek into the pleasant weather on the open prairie. The warming sun was comfortable in contrast to the harsh winter they'd endured in barracks.

Guy DuBose had dispersed his troops in a subtle formation that gave them a full view of the area where the colonel would hold his conference with the Chogolas. Each man's single-shot carbine was loaded, and their revolvers had five of the cylinder compartments full of ball and powder. For safety's sake, the hammers rested on the empty chamber to lessen the chance of accidental firing.

Lieutenant Robertson pulled a cheroot from his tunic pocket. He bit off the end and lit it, staring straight over where Lame Elk now squatted in the

53

agency yard. He exhaled the first mouthful of smoke. "There is a savage that will be the cause of all our troubles this summer."

"Yes, sir," Guy agreed. "But perhaps Talks-To-Them can keep a lid on things."

"We just issued a short ration of beef," Robertson reminded him. "Combine that with the Comanche warriors' natural restlessness and love of adventure, Sergeant DuBose. Do you think the old chief can keep those bucks under control?"

Guy didn't answer. He fished in his own pockets for one of the cheap cigars he'd purchased at the sutler's the last payday. After touching a match to the tobacco, he smoked languidly and slowly, savoring the luxury of having nothing to do. Now and then he glanced over toward the agency store where Netta Druce stood with her husband.

The sun continued in its arc, the mid-morning heat now increasing across the silent people waiting in the agency yard.

CHAPTER 5

The scene around the agency had settled into a sullen silence that was finally broken when a distant trumpeter sounded *Assembly*. The notes echoed in hollow tones over the open plains country. Within moments a mounted color guard appeared, led by the musician. Guy ordered his men to attention and gave the command to present arms. The Indians perked up, turning their eyes toward the sight.

The instrument again sounded the call. The group rode into the dusty yard. There were four riders: one carried the national flag, one the regimental colors, and two acted as armed escorts on the flanks. They circled around one time, then galloped back to the entrance, and came to a halt.

Several minutes later, Col. O. David Gatley, the regimental commander, made a dignified appearance flanked by his adjutant and the sergeant major.

This grand entrance was not official protocol. It was done because the Indians loved to see some sort of ceremony at the start of any talks between themselves and the white men. Even Lame Elk, in a bad temper most of the time, was impressed by the flags and the loud instruments that made so much noise.

Talks-To-Them walked forward and held up his right hand. "Hello to you, Gatley," he greeted.

The colonel smiled and waved from horseback. "How are you today, Talks-To-Them?"

"We will sit down," the old chief said. "I will tell you what is in my heart."

"And I will tell you what is in mine," Gatley said. "But first we must listen to Palmer Druce. He has called for this meeting." The officer waited for one of the troopers to scamper forward and take his reins. Only then did he swing out of the saddle.

Both Druce and his wife came down from the agency store to greet the colonel. "How do you do, sir?"

"I am fine, thank you, Mister Druce," Gatley answered. He bowed elegantly to Mrs. Druce. "My compliments, ma'am."

"It is so nice to have you visit again, Colonel," Netta Druce said. "Even if the situation is more business than pleasure."

"Thank you," Gatley said. He was in a hurry. There were numerous administrative tasks waiting for him back at Fort Alexander. He called over to Talks-To-Them. "Do you want to go over to the Talking Place?" This was an area under a pecan tree that sat like a lone sentinel some twenty yards away from the agency buildings.

"Yes," the old Comanche answered. "I think there is much to say."

The entire group, with Guy's men following at a respectful distance with the color guard, moved across the yard. They formed themselves up along the north side of the area while Colonel Gatley, his adjutant, Lieutenant Robertson, Talks-To-Them, and Lame Elk sat down. Mrs. Druce withdrew out of deference to the Indians' feelings, since they would welcome no women at what they considered an important affair. The remainder of the Chogolas, numbering eleven warriors, settled down on the opposite side of the soldiers.

Chairs were set out for the army officers and Palmer Druce, but the Indians, including old Talks-To-Them, preferred to sit on blankets thrown on the ground. When all were ready, Colonel Gatley opened the ceremony.

"Talks-To-Them," he said. "I greet you. After last summer's troubles, we have had a quiet and peaceful winter. I hope the situation continues into this year's warmer seasons."

Talks-To-Them said nothing. But he did stand up to signify acceptance of the greetings then sat down again beside Lame Elk.

"I am here," continued the colonel, "because of a request by Mr. Druce. He feels things are not right here at the agency. I will ask him to speak to all of us on what troubles him."

Druce stood up and spoke facing down between the two groups. His hawkish face appeared strained and worried. "I am unhappy with Lame Elk," he stated bluntly. "I did not tell the soldiers about this before, but he left the agency three times during the winter. I admonished him for breaking the treaty. Also, on numerous occasions he has come into the agency store and made threats. He has boasted that he and his Hawks-of-the-Wind are going to Texas and kill white people. He told me that he will be gone all this summer, then come back in late fall for the cows the U.S. government will give him. If he talked alone like this I would not care. But I have heard him telling other Indians of these diabolical plans. He is a bad influence and I want him arrested."

Lame Elk, his expression cold and neutral, sat staring straight ahead as if there were no other persons around him.

Gatley motioned to Talks-To-Them. "Lame Elk has done this before. You told me you would talk to him."

The old man stood up again. "Yes, Colonel Gatley. I have spoken to him and told him to stop making trouble. But he will not listen to me. Neither will any of the young men. The cattle promised us did not last through the winter. We went hungry and when I spoke to Mister Druce he said there was nothing to be done until the next shipment arrived. When the people are hungry and angry, my words do not mean anything. You must help me. I will have no control over the young men if you don't."

Now Lame Elk reacted. He laughed aloud.

"You see?" Talks-To-Them said. "I am mocked and insulted because the people are hungry. Where are the cattle?"

"We just issued you cattle," the colonel said.

"But will they last until the next time?" Talks-To-Them asked. "We cannot count. Our language does not put numbers on them like the white man. But when I look at the cows the U.S. gives us, I pretend it is a buffalo herd. I say to myself if that would be enough buffalo to feed us for three moons. I say to myself it is not enough, the people will go hungry again. They will think I am foolish."

"You must learn to make the cattle last," Gatley admonished him. "Even now as I rode up, I could hear the bellow of many of them being slaughtered."

"Yes," Talks-To-Them agreed. "Because the people are hungry. They want to eat."

Gatley realized argument was useless. He turned his attention to Lame Elk. "What do you say to all this?"

Lame Elk stood up. He was a tall, dignified man the color of dark copper. Well-built and muscular, his eyes had a special piercing quality that made him appear as dangerous in intellect as he would be physically. "There is too much talk."

"That is how men settle things," Gatley said smugly.

"The white man told us that if we stayed at the agency, we would be given cattle to eat," Lame Elk said. "We do not get enough cattle to last us. You say, 'Don't eat so much so fast.' I say, 'Your counsel is as empty as our bellies.' Why should I stay here and be hungry when I can ride out and kill buffalo and eat good? It is true I left the agency this winter. But I didn't kill white people. I killed buffalo and brought the meat back. That stupid old Talks-To-Them sits in his lodge and repeats your words to the people. The words mean nothing. I give them meat. Pretty soon you must seek me and not to Talks-To-Them if you want to find out about the Chogola Comanches."

Colonel Gatley returned the Indian's cold gaze. "What about the things you said to Mr. Druce?"

"Am I supposed to tremble because that man-woman tells you what I say?" Lame Elk asked defiantly. "All he wants to do is take our men-children and turn them into women to scrape at the ground and

59

throw seeds down to grow. He wants them to know the markings on paper. I do not like this. Now he wants you to take me away and lock me in a building." He paused to glare at the colonel. "Will you do this?"

Gatley wisely shook his head. "No, Lame Elk. I can see no point in doing such a thing even if you did say bad things."

Lame Elk's voice grew in intensity. "I am a warrior! If I want to go to Texas with my Hawks-of-the-Wind and kill white people, I will do so. I am not afraid of you or your soldiers."

"You must control your anger," Gatley said. "Let us not talk of killing each other. Let us talk of peace and living together like brothers."

This began a half hour of declarations, accusations, and boasting that bounced among the three main speakers. Colonel Gatley spoke strongly in behalf of the United States Government's position. Talks-To-Them accused both the government and the army of making it impossible for him to maintain control over his tribe. Lame Elk damned them all, and let everyone know that he would do as he pleased. Palmer Druce blamed everyone for the problems and complained bitterly of how they were all making his life as complicated and miserable as Talks-To-Them's.

"How can my wife and I teach their children if you allow Lame Elk to poison their minds against us?" Druce asked Gatley. "I want you to keep soldiers here on the agency at all times."

"I could only spare a few," Colonel Gatley told him. "We have other duties besides the agency."

"I will appreciate any help at all," Druce said.

Nothing was settled, but Colonel Gatley ended the

session with a stern warning to Lame Elk.

"If you leave the agency and commit crimes of murder and pillage, the soldiers will come after you. They will capture you and bring you back here for punishment. That is all I have to say."

The meeting broke up, and the Indians drifted back toward their lodges. Druce, however, did feel better now that Lame Elk had gotten at least a minor dressing down. "I wish to thank you for your efforts, Colonel. Perhaps that evil man will heed your warning and behave himself."

Gatley, who would be up to his neck in a bloody conflict if Lame Elk didn't obey his words, spoke sincerely. "My fervent hope is also for peace, Mr. Druce. There is nothing to be gained by anyone if a full-blown Indian war breaks out."

"Of course," Druce said. "My wife has prepared some fresh coffee and cake, Colonel. Would you honor us with a visit before you return to Fort Alexander?"

"Yes, thank you, Palmer," Gatley said. "But first I must speak with one of my soldiers. I shall join you and your wife presently."

He strode over to the section where Guy DuBose stood. "Good day to you, Sergeant," he said taking the other's salute.

"How do you do, sir," Guy responded.

"Let's take a stroll, Sergeant," Gatley said. "I would very much like a word with you." The two walked slowly away from the pecan tree. "Your new company commander will be here next week."

"That will be good news for Captain Wayne," Guy said. "He's been waiting for the first opportunity to retire."

Gatley nodded. Suddenly he stopped and looked at the sergeant. An expression of exasperation clouded his face. "By damn, DuBose, why did you have to fight for the Confederacy?"

"I am a South Carolinian, sir," Guy responded surprised.

Gatley continued to look at the other man. "I could use you as an officer, Sergeant. But you know that's impossible since you served the southern cause."

"I would be surprised otherwise, sir," Guy stated.

"This new officer is straight out of the War Department, did you know that?" Gatley asked.

"Yes, sir," DuBose replied. "I'd heard he must have lost in some political maneuvering."

Gatley laughed. "He certainly did! He chose the wrong brigadier general in a struggle for a departmental command. The fellow's rivals in the adjutant general's branch went after his backers with a vengeance. His bad judgement cost him a soft job and banishment out here to us."

Guy displayed a cynical smile. "It makes one wonder about our own true situation, doesn't it?"

"I've never wondered about it," Gatley said. "But we can expect a bitter, inexperienced man to deal with. I'll be relying heavily on you to help him along."

"Our first sergeant will certainly—"

"Oh, damn McClary's eyes!" Gatley snapped. "He's a good enough administrative man, but in the field he's a useless sot. Your friend Sergeant Tate is a good soldier, but he's a bit dull-witted. So it'll be up to you to see that our banished aristocrat is helped along."

"I appreciate your confidence in me, sir," Guy said.

"You heard what Lame Elk said, of course," Gatley

added. "And you know what that means."

"I expect a repeat of last summer, sir," Guy replied. "We'll have plenty of unpleasant activity to occupy us."

"Indeed," Gatley said. "Well, I'm off to visit the Druces. I will continue to take you into my confidence until we see what sort of officer the new captain is. Be perfectly candid with me, DuBose. I'll need that from you in the trying days ahead."

"Yes, sir," Guy said. He saluted the departing colonel, then turned his attention to getting his men back to Fort Alexander.

CHAPTER 6

An atmosphere of tension settled over Fort Alexander. Everywhere on post, from Soap Suds Row up to the officers' quarters, they spoke in worried tones of the coming summer. No one expected Lame Elk and his followers to remain docile reservation Indians for much longer.

Attention from the threat of Indian war was diverted momentarily with the arrival of Capt. Gordon Blackburn. Curiosity about the new officer had fueled several rumors about him. The story that he was a disgraced dandy who'd done a powerful politician's daughter wrong was circulating in the non-commissioned community. Officers Row was more dignified and logical. The tale there was that he'd made a horrible blunder in the quartermaster department that had cost the government hundreds of thousands of dollars.

The subject of all this talk finally made his appearance three days after the meeting with Talks-To-Them and Lame Elk.

An ambulance wagon had been dispatched to the railhead at Dahlquart to pick him up at the depot. These vehicles were the most comfortable to ride in when crossing the rough open country of the prairie. Built with strong springs to absorb the jolts and shocks, they also offered a more pleasant interior for the passengers.

When the Fort Alexander ambulance arrived in Dahlquart, the driver and guard found a dusty, ill-tempered passenger waiting for them. After enduring a petulant tongue-lashing for tardiness and their unkempt appearance, the two soldiers loaded the passenger's several trunks into the back of the vehicle.

Captain Blackburn's mood had not improved a bit when he finally arrived at post headquarters and presented a copy of his orders to Lieutenant Harris, the regimental adjutant.

Harris, a hardworking officer in his early thirties, gave the documents a quick going over before passing them to the sergeant major for filing. "We've been expecting you—that is, an officer for assignment—for more than a year, sir."

Blackburn, unsmiling, slapped at the dust on his uniform. "I am not surprised that there are unfilled posts in this regiment." He was a short, stout man with thick black mutton chop whiskers. His hair was thinning perceptibly on top, but his eyebrows were thick and full, growing together across his forehead and giving him the appearance of a permanent frown.

"I'm sure the colonel will want to have a word with you, Captain," Lieutenant Harris said.

"I am a brevet lieutenant colonel," Blackburn informed him in a gruff voice.

"Yes, sir," Harris said. "It's in your records. Just a moment, please." The adjutant went to a door marked *Commanding Officer,* and knocked. He stepped inside without waiting for a reply from the interior. Seconds later he emerged. "The colonel will see you now."

Blackburn stuck his kepi under his arm and marched through the door. He drew himself up short before the desk and saluted. "Sir, Brevet Lieutenant Colonel Gordon Blackburn is pleased to report for duty."

"How do you do, Captain," Colonel Gatley said. "Welcome to Fort Alexander. How was your trip?"

"Dirty and maddening after leaving the East," Blackburn said. He was again annoyed by this oversight of his brevet rank.

"I fear there is a great lack of luxuries on this side of the Mississippi, Captain," Colonel Gatley said.

"I am a brevet lieutenant colonel," Blackburn said to set the record straight once and for all.

"I suppose the adjutant should have told you, but my policy within this regiment is to ignore brevet ranks. They are very confusing and even disruptive. It would be ridiculous to have a captain who was a brevet lieutenant colonel under the command of a major who was a brevet nothing, wouldn't it?"

Blackburn's eyes widened. He was used to Washington City military politics where one used every advantage to the hilt, whether it be medals or brevet ranks. "Yes, sir."

Gatley took a hard look at the new officer. He could see the bitterness, disappointment, and dismay behind the facade of soldierly correctness. He felt sorry for the man. "You'll be taking command of C Company, Captain. The commander is a veteran by the name of

Wayne. Frankly, he hasn't been of much use to me during the past two years."

"I presume the company will have to be brought up to high standards of discipline and efficiency," Blackburn remarked.

"That, at least, will not be a problem for you," Gatley said in a soothing tone. "The first sergeant is a hard-drinker, but he keeps the records up to date and correct. The two sergeants, DuBose and Tate, are damned good soldiers and leaders. I think you should know that both are ex-Confederates. Tate was an N.C.O. in a regiment of Georgia volunteers, while DuBose was a captain in one of the better South Carolina regiments."

"There are no qualified N.C.O.s who were loyal to their country during the last war, sir?" Blackburn asked.

"You'll find them both reliable and faithful, Captain," Colonel Gatley said. "Sergeant DuBose, in particular, is an excellent leader."

Blackburn's scowl increased. "Then I am being saddled with rebels. What about the lieutenants?"

"There are none, Captain Blackburn," Colonel Gatley said. "The regiment is severely undermanned."

"I find that distressing," Blackburn said.

"Not as much as I," Gatley said. "We're stretched pretty thin. Our principal duties are law enforcement and maintaining control over the Chogola Comanches. There is a lot of patrolling involved in both instances. So you should plan on long periods away from home. I understand you are married."

"Yes, sir," Blackburn replied. "My wife will join me at the earliest convenience. There was much to do in closing out our home and packing away our furniture and other effects."

Gatley wondered if Blackburn was one of those few lucky officers who fit into the category of having money on the "outside." He decided to probe. "It will be terribly costly to ship many things out here, Captain."

"We do not plan to bring everything, Colonel," Blackburn said with a near haughty tone in his voice. "The great majority of our belongings is being placed in storage until my return to the War Department."

Gatley felt a flash of anger. "Evidently, Captain, you do not think you'll be long in the regiment."

"I do not, sir."

"In that case, we shouldn't waste time in getting you to active duty," Gatley said. He spoke loudly toward the door. "Lieutenant Harris!"

The adjutant quickly appeared. "Yes, sir?"

"Be so kind as to conduct Captain Blackburn to C Company, will you, please?"

"Yes, sir."

"You will be very busy, Captain Blackburn," the colonel said. "I strongly suggest you take advantage of your company's most excellent non-commissioned officers."

"I shall take that into serious consideration, sir," Blackburn said.

Gatley looked at the captain and now saw something else in the man he'd failed to notice before: arrogance. "You are dismissed, Captain Blackburn."

Harris led Blackburn out of the building and across the parade ground. They walked in silence for several moments before the captain finally spoke. "I say,

Harris. I would have appreciated it if you would have informed me that brevet ranks were not honored in this regiment."

"I'm sure you would have," Harris said with a slight smile.

"I felt rather stupid having the colonel tell me so," Blackburn fumed.

"Really? I apologize, Captain," Lieutenant Harris said. "But one tends to forget certain protocol when such situations as Indian raids, massacres of civilians, and other unpleasant happenings clutter up the duty day."

They continued down to the orderly room, stopping at one that had the C Company guidon planted in front of the door. Harris knocked and stepped inside.

First Sgt. Edward McClary leaped to his feet and stood at attention. Across from him, a gray-haired, paunchy captain of fifty-six years of age, slumped at his desk. His plump face was haggard, and he appeared to be physically ill. The smell of stale liquor hung like an invisible cloud around him. He got unsteadily to his feet and looked past Harris at the stranger. "Is this my replacement?"

"It is, Captain Wayne. Allow me to present Captain Blackburn."

Wayne offered his hand. "Dan Wayne at your service."

"Gordon Blackburn," said the new arrival.

"I presume you are anxious to jump into the fray, Captain Blackburn," Wayne said.

"I am."

"Good," he said. He gestured to McClary. "Get the company records out, Sergeant."

"Yes, sir." McClary crossed the room and grabbed an armful of file boxes and memo books. He set them down on his desk. "Here they are, sir. The comp'ny order book, letters received and index, letters sent and index, sick report book, morning report book, duty roster—"

"I am well aware of company records," Blackburn said coldly.

"Yes, sir!" McClary snapped.

Wayne stood up and walked around his desk, sitting down on it. "Help yourself, Blackburn."

Blackburn gave the documents a quick but thoroughly professional perusal. He found them all neat and up-to-date. "They seem to be in order," he said.

"Thank you, sir," McClary said proudly.

"I smell liquor on your breath," Blackburn said. "Have you been drinking, Sergeant?"

Captain Wayne interrupted. "We both have."

Blackburn smiled slightly and continued to look at McClary. "During my tenure as company commander, you will not drink on duty, Sergeant."

"Yes, sir!"

Wayne smirked. "After a few years you'll find a nip or two will help you get through the tedium, Captain Blackburn. That is something we have plenty of— tedium. It fits in nicely with the winter snow, the summer heat and flies, the endless routine of doing the same damned thing over and over and over. Tedium. Tedium. Tedium."

Blackburn snapped his disapproving gaze to Wayne. "How long have you been in the army, Captain?"

"Thirty-six years," Wayne answered. He tapped his shoulder straps bearing the double bars of captain.

71

"With twenty-four of them spent in this exalted rank." He laughed. "I would be willing to wager I've worn out dozens of these insignia."

Blackburn gave the records on McClary's desk another glance, then turned away. "I shall be back tomorrow for the transfer of property, Captain Wayne." He looked at McClary. "I will also speak with the two other N.C.O.s, Sergeant."

"Yes, sir."

"Now," he said to Lieutenant Harris. "I would like to go to my quarters."

"Yes, sir," Harris answered. "The quartermaster sergeant has seen that your trunks were taken care of. You've ranked the Robertsons out of quarters, but since Captain Wayne is leaving shortly and you'll be having his billets, I thought you would not mind taking one of the empty subalterns' houses. That way Lieutenant Robertson and his wife won't have to go through an unnecessary move."

"That won't do at all," Blackburn said. "Have whatever quarters I am entitled to prepared immediately."

Harris' jaw locked in rage, but he kept a lid on his feelings, "Yes, sir, Captain Blackburn!"

CHAPTER 7

Sergeants Guy DuBose and Harry Tate stood at the barracks door looking down the twin rows of troopers standing by their respective bunks. The men of Company C had gone through an early, critical inspection by the two N.C.O.s. All discrepancies found by the meticulous sergeants had been quickly corrected. Now the soldiers stood tall and sharp, ready to begin the new day under the command of Capt. Gordon Blackburn.

The rising sun's pinkish glow cast through the barracks windows, was drowned out by the lights of the lanterns hanging from the squad room ceiling.

"Remember!" Guy announced loudly. "This is the first reveille with the new company commander. We don't want him to think that he's been handed a gang of tramps. You are soldiers in the regular army, so show him how smart we can turn out for formation."

Tate growled, "And I'll kick anybody's ass that moves slow and sloppy."

Even the brawler Pvt. Tim Donovan would pay heed

to that statement. Sgt. Harry Tate was known to back up his orders with fists and boots when his temper snapped. The men, a bit nervous but standing stock still, gave the sergeants their strictest attention.

The urgent notes of *Reveille* suddenly sounded. "Outside! Outside!" Guy ordered.

"Perk up, damn you!" Tate added.

The young cavalrymen rushed through the door into the semi-darkness and immediately fell into the proper company formation outside. Guy, as senior sergeant, took over and marched them all up the street between the barracks until giving them a column movement in front of the row of orderly rooms. After moving the soldiers into formation with the regiment's other companies, he brought both sections to a halt and faced them toward their waiting first sergeant.

"Parade, rest!" Guy commanded.

Each man moved his right foot six inches to the rear while clasping his hands in front of his body. The two sections, their left legs slightly bent at the knee, presented a picture of soldierly silence and steadiness of position. McClary smiled to himself, knowing that DuBose and Tate had taken extra pains that morning.

Captain Gordon Blackburn, who had been standing in the orderly room door, moved to his position behind the troop.

First Sergeant McClary now took over. "Comp'nee, a-tin-hut!" he commanded. There was a loud crack as heels clicked in unison and smart slaps of hands along the seams of the light blue trousers. "Section leaders, ree-port!"

"First Section two men absent, one man regimental guard, seventeen men present for duty," Guy reported

74

with a salute.

"Second Section," Sgt. Harry Tate yelled, "three men absent, two men sick, sixteen men present for duty."

"Parade rest!" McClary yelled. He waited for Captain Blackburn to begin his march around to the front of the company. "Comp'nee, a-tin-hut!" When the captain had walked to his rear, the first sergeant made an about face and saluted. "Sir, five men absent, two men sick, one man regimental guard, thirty-three men present for duty." He, as the first sergeant who did the morning reports, already knew the exact count before Guy or Tate had made their own reports.

Blackburn didn't seem to notice the men's smartness in the increasing daylight. He glowered at the company, then turned to face the major at the front of the squadron. At the proper command, the captain passed on the daily status report to the squadron commander who, after tallying the four companies in First Squadron, yelled the strength report up to the regimental commander.

A flurry of orders, salutes, and facing movements were passed back down until the company commanders again took over their men.

Blackburn scowled. "Dismiss the company, Sergeant. I will see all sergeants immediately."

"Yes, sir." McClary correctly followed the ritual with another salute. After waiting for the officer to march away, he again turned and faced the company. "Section leaders, take charge of your sections and dismiss 'em. Sergeants report to the orderly room immediately."

After making sure the corporals would take over and

supervise the pre-breakfast chores around the barracks, Guy and Tate went to the orderly room. As they walked through the door, McClary looked at them and rolled his eyes in consternation as a signal that all was not well.

Blackburn, sitting behind his desk, lit a pipe. He smoked slowly, staring at the sergeants without speaking for several long moments. Finally he said, "Well? What about those absences?"

Guy and Tate, puzzled, looked at each other.

"God damn it!" Blackburn exploded. "Are the senior N.C.O.s in this miserable company a trio of idiots? McClary gave me the same stupid looks you two just displayed."

"I don't understand, sir," Guy said.

"Let me put it simply, Sergeant," Blackburn said. "Why do we have men absent? Are they on detached duty? Or perhaps, they have social engagements somewhere and are unable to attend reveille? Is that it?"

"Sir," Guy said. "The five men have deserted the army. Three went separately, but two left together. They have been gone for less than thirty days. After that much time they officially become deserters and are removed from the company rolls. Until then we are required to carry them on our reports."

"For God's sake!" Blackburn exploded. "Has any effort been made to track them down and bring them back?"

Tate, who had been quiet, nodded enthusiastically. "Oh, yes, sir! We chased after 'em each and ever'time, but them rascals planned it out too good. They was long gone afore we knowed about it. Most o' the time they run away on a Sunday after Church Call. We don't even know they've hightailed it 'til Call To Quarters that night. Then it's too dark to trail 'em. The earliest we can send out patrols is after Monday reveille."

"Did they take any government property?" Blackburn asked.

"Two of them took their government issue carbines, sir," Guy said. "I presume this was for protection against Indians and criminal whites. Of course, they were wearing uniforms, so the clothing can be considered misappropriated."

"This is a black eye to this company!" Blackburn snapped.

"Sir, all the companies in the regiment have had deserters," Guy said. "I am afraid to say that this is not at all an unusual situation."

"That's right, sir," McClary interjected. "The sergeant major told me that at least a third o' the men has taken off."

Blackburn was silent for several moments before he spoke. "I do not care what the standards are in other companies. Such outrageous conduct cannot be tolerated. It costs the government a considerable sum to recruit, equip, and train soldiers. To have the scalawags run away at the slightest excuse is completely unacceptable." He paused and eyed the N.C.O.s to judge their reaction to his words. Then he added, "If any other man in this company deserts, I will hold his section sergeant responsible for the unhappy affair. Perhaps removing a few chevrons will shape up this miserable company." He glared at them through the thick smoke from his pipe. "You are dismissed." He waited for the two line sergeants to leave before speaking to McClary. "Where is Captain Wayne?"

"Prob'ly in his quarters asleep, sir," McClary said.

"The drunken—" He checked himself, not wanting to belittle a fellow officer in front of an enlisted man. "Does he often miss reveille?"

"He *always* misses reveille, sir," McClary said.

"I see. No matter. As long as we can wrap up the transfer of command today." He got up and took his kepi off the hat rack by the door. "I am going to see the quartermaster, Sergeant McClary. I will be back as soon as my business with him is completed."

Blackburn left the orderly room and strode across the parade ground toward regimental headquarters. It was broad daylight by then, and the bright sun in the sky promised a pleasant day.

When he arrived at his destination, Blackburn wasted no time in going to the quartermaster's office. "Lieutenant Robertson?"

Robertson, who had been forced with his wife to move from their quarters when Blackburn refused to stay a few days in a small subaltern billet, fought down his anger at the captain's unexpected appearance. "Yes, sir?"

"What are the arrangements for officers to mess?" Blackburn asked.

Robertson started to answer when his wife appeared at the door. "Good morning," she called out. When she saw Blackburn she excused herself. "Oh, dear, I'm sorry. I thought you were alone, Bill."

Blackburn turned toward her and effected a bow. "Madam."

Robertson reluctantly introduced them. "Captain Blackburn, this is my wife."

Minnie Robertson's smile was pleasant though not warm. "How do you do, Captain."

"Your servant, madam."

Minnie Robertson looked at her husband. "I just dropped by to remind you that the Harrises will be having dinner with us, so don't work late tonight."

"I'll see that I don't," Robertson replied. He turned his attention back to Blackburn. "To answer your question, Captain Blackburn, there are no special arrangements for officers to mess. We take our meals in our quarters." He gave Blackburn a special look. "You do have an excellent stove in your new home."

"Lieutenant, I do not cook," Blackburn said.

"There is a back room at the sutler's store for officers," Robertson said. "A rather simple luncheon fare is available there for mid-day eating."

"Captain Blackburn," Minnie Robertson said. "You are welcome to join Lieutenant and Mrs. Harris in dining with us this evening. If you wish, you may share our table until your wife arrives or other arrangements can be made."

"I don't wish to inconvenience you, madam," Blackburn said. "I would prefer to hire a lady to serve as a cook and housekeeper."

"I know of a young girl who would do just fine," Mrs. Robertson said. "I'm sure she will be pleased to work for you until your wife arrives."

"I desire a domestic on a permanent basis," Blackburn said.

The Robertsons immediately realized the Blackburns had more to live on than just army pay. Minnie Robertson said, "The girl is looking for work, I know, since Captain Wayne is leaving."

"I will interview her," Blackburn said. "Where can she be found?"

"As a matter of fact, she is Sergeant Tate's oldest daughter. I'll see she comes to see you," Mrs. Robertson said. "In the meantime, we would still enjoy your company at dinner tonight. I shall serve after retreat."

"Most grateful, madam. I am pleased to accept your kind invitation. Good day to you. Good day, Lieutenant." Now, knowing that he would not be able to eat until noon at the sutler's store, Blackburn's mood and his stomach both grumbled as he returned to the company.

Guy DuBose and Harry Tate had each taken their respective sections and were deeply engrossed in dismounted drill when Blackburn came back. Rather than go into the orderly room, Blackburn spent the next ten minutes watching his new command go through their paces. He summoned the two sergeants to his presence. The two N.C.O.s turned their men over to the senior corporals and reported to the captain.

"That is the sorriest example of marching I have seen in more than twenty years in the army," Blackburn said.

Both Guy and Tate were angered and surprised by the remark. They took a great deal of pride in their men's ability on the drill field. Guy, particularly, was irritated. He spoke respectfully but firmly. "Sir, our company won the regimental drill trophy two years running. In fact it is in the orderly room on the shelf above Sergeant McClary's desk."

"I don't care a whit about some prize won out here in the wilderness, Sergeant DuBose," Blackburn said.

80

"And I don't like the tone in your voice."

"I apologize, sir."

Blackburn glared at Guy. "I am told you were an officer in the rebel army. Is that true?"

"Yes, sir."

"Are you a West Pointer by any chance, Sergeant?"

"No, sir," Guy answered.

"I thought not," the captain sneered. He turned his dark, disapproving gaze on Tate. "And you were a Johnny Reb too, were you not?"

"Georgia volunteers, sir."

"I didn't ask what pack of traitors you belonged to," Blackburn said. "And I don't care. I have not been favorably impressed by you two so far. Let me warn you that I will not tolerate slackness in non-commissioned officers like Captain Wayne evidently has done. Do you understand?"

"Yes, sir," they replied in unison.

"Now let's return to the drill field, and see if those Bowery boys of yours can begin displaying some sort of soldierly conduct!"

The two sergeants, with the captain following, went back to their sections. Guy, controlling his rage, urged his men to concentrate on each movement as he coached them along as subtly as he could under Blackburn's dark gaze. Tate, on the other hand, turned into a tyrant as he bullied and cursed at his men in an attempt to sharpen their marching.

When *Officers Call* was blown and Blackburn had to report to regimental headquarters, both N.C.O.s felt the heavy weight of injustice lifted from their broad shoulders.

Officers Call, called daily by the adjutant, was a time

for these gentlemen of the regiment to gather and communicate. The official and latest news from higher headquarters and their own commanding colonel was given them by Lieutenant Harris. In turn, they discussed the day-to-day problems they faced in performing their jobs. Between arguments and protests, the business of the army was brought into sharper focus and immediate problems were quickly solved—usually with the ranking man getting his prerogatives.

Blackburn was introduced to the other officers. His reception was decidedly cold. The fact that he had forced the Robertsons to make a totally unnecessary and inconvenient move did not gain favor among the close-knit community. He was fully aware of this unfriendliness, but he was not bothered by it. Blackburn remained silent, keeping his contempt for these cavalry officers to himself.

Lieutenant Harris, the adjutant, wrapped up the meeting with a warning. "Mr. Druce has again sent word of bad behavior by Lame Elk," he said. "Colonel Gatley fears that this summer may be even more active and bloodier than last year. He wants me to urge you to stay flexible and keep your commands at the utmost readiness for any situations."

Blackburn listened to the last announcement with more than a little interest. He was thoughtful for several moments. There were two opportunities open to him to get back to the War Department and a good staff appointment. The political infighting in the military bureaucracy could go his way, but that was doubtful. On the other hand, it wouldn't hurt to be mentioned in dispatches and garner some favorable publicity in the eastern newspapers. It was a well known fact that the brash and pushy Lt. Col. George Armstrong Custer was doing that very thing with his 7th Cavalry Regiment.

Lieutenant Harris finally brought the meeting to a close with an announcement that lantern wicks for the officers' quarters could no longer be drawn from the quartermaster. They would have to be purchased. With Officers Call completed, Blackburn left at the earliest opportunity. The other officers remained for a few private conversations before going to their quarters for lunch.

Blackburn went to the sutler's store for his own meal. A couple of subalterns who didn't have the responsibility to answer Officers Call were already there in the room set aside for the commissioned elite. Blackburn nodded to them as he walked up to the food counter. They acknowledged his presence with terse "Good afternoons" then went back to their conversation.

The captain found the fare severely limited. A smoked ham, a large slab of cheese that had obviously had the mold carved off it, and government bread that Dawkins the sutler had bought from the post bakery made up the meager menu. After fashioning a rather dry sandwich and getting a cup of coffee, he went to a table to consume the tasteless meal. The lieutenants glanced over at him several times, but made no effort to speak. Blackburn, at least, appreciated that. He finished the worst meal he'd had in his entire army career, paid the dollar price, and left.

When Blackburn returned to the orderly room, he found Capt. Dan Wayne waiting for him. The officer, bleary-eyed and reeking of whiskey, sat at his old desk. He had looked bad to Blackburn the first time he met him, but the old captain's appearance that afternoon was pathetic. He was a sick man, beaten down by long years of heavy drinking and hard soldiering under the severest circumstances.

"Good day, Cap'n Blackburn," he greeted.

"Good afternoon," Blackburn replied. "I trust you are ready for the transfer of property."

"I am as ready as I'll ever be," Wayne conceded. He waggled a finger at McClary. "Got those property books?"

"Yes, sir."

Wayne struggled to his feet. "Let's get this over with. It'll take the rest of the afternoon to count every locker box, bunk, carbine, and all those etceteras." He laughed without humor. "The etceteras take the longest, don't they?"

"I suppose," Blackburn said coldly. "We would have been done by now if we'd tended to the business in the morning."

"My dear, sir!" Wayne exclaimed. "I was too damned drunk earlier today. A man in his cups—even an officer and gentleman—cannot be expected to tally accurately, can he?" He motioned to McClary. "Lead on, oh faithful sergeant, and take us through this dreary process."

"Yes, sir," McClary said. "Let's start with the barracks. That's gonna take the longest."

As they followed the N.C.O., Wayne spoke to his fellow officer. "You realize, of course, that I have been completely at the mercy of the first sergeant. We'll find out from this inventory if he's borne me any ill will over these years we've served together."

McClary grinned with an impish light in his eyes.

They began the ordeal by counting the mops and brooms hung neatly beside the barracks door. The long afternoon dwindled into a dreary routine of counting objects, then seeing if the tally matched what was in the property books. When the job was finally finished, Wayne fairly sparkled.

"By God, Sergeant McClary, you've done right by me!"

"Yes, sir," McClary said smiling.

"There's not as much as an india rubber eraser missing, you rascal!" Wayne exclaimed.

"You was an officer that had our respect and good feelings, sir," McClary said. "I reckon you know that more'n a few of us old soljers is sad to see you go." He turned toward Blackburn, his face now cold and expressionless. "Are you ready to sign for the comp'ny property now, sir?"

Blackburn knew he'd have to keep his eye on both the first sergeant and every piece of government property listed in those books.

CHAPTER 8

Martha Tate, standing at her kitchen counter, filled the two tin cups with boiling coffee. She carried them outside, giving one to her husband Harry, and the other to Guy DuBose. The pair of sergeants sat in front of the Tate quarters enjoying the warm spring evening.

"Thank you for the supper, Mrs. Tate," Guy said sincerely. "It was delicious."

"I'm pleased you liked it, Mister DuBose," Martha replied.

"Where did you get those black-eyed peas?" Guy asked. "What a nice surprise. I don't believe I have had the opportunity to eat any for more than three years."

Harry Tate grinned. "I knew you'd be surprised."

"I even had Laura Lee take some over to cook for Cap'n Blackburn," Martha said.

"A sad waste o' good southern food on a northern stummick," Harry growled.

Their oldest daughter, fifteen-year-old Laura Lee, made extra money by working as a housekeeper and cook for various families among the officers. Mrs.

Robertson, the quartermaster's wife, had fetched her for employment in the Blackburn household.

"I bought 'em off that peddler that was through here a coupla days ago," Martha replied. "We'd had you over sooner, but since Cap'n Blackburn has kept you so busy, we din't have a chance."

"That sonofabitch," Harry said in calm tone, "is no good Yankee scum."

"You'd better watch your choice of adjectives," Guy warned. "Don't forget you're serving in the Yankee army yourself now."

"I don't know what a ad-jek-tif is," Harry responded. "But if that's what Blackburn is, so be it."

Martha, who had stayed nearby, spoke to them from the door. "At least the men in the comp'ny have their evenings free again."

Blackburn had decreed that every soldier in C Company would be confined to the barracks for an unspecified amount of time. To make matters worse, the captain saw to it that the evenings in quarters were made even more miserable by conducting numerous inspections of the strictest nature. He meticulously went over carbines, sabers, boots, accouterments, and the billets themselves. The slightest infraction or smudge brought immediate punishment to the offender.

The penalty for these infractions was an old army punishment. Rain barrels were rolled from their places at the bottom of the drain pipes of the barracks' rain gutters. Those who failed the inspections had to stand on the barrel rims while holding their carbines above their heads. It was a difficult and painful feat. Those forced into it were quickly brought to the point of exhaustion from cramped shoulder and calf muscles. A couple had sustained bad injuries when they fainted and fell to the ground.

After three days of the routine, Guy finally protested. But he did so in a respectful, proper manner. He wanted to avoid any indication that minor sedition was in the making. Guy waited until there were no other troops around when he finally approached Captain Blackburn. "Sir," he said to the officer in a calm tone. "I think we've reached the limit. Whatever lesson you're imparting has surely been learned now."

"The reasons behind this extra discipline seem to escape even you, Sergeant DuBose," Blackburn had replied. "The message to this scum is that I am not an officer who will tolerate any breach of the regulations. I demand the utmost in conduct and efficiency."

"They understand that, sir," Guy replied. "And I beg your pardon, but this company has always been the best in the regiment."

"Perhaps so, but that does not matter. I do not consider this regiment the *best* in the army. The top dogs of a pack of curs have no reason for pride. These aren't honorable soldiers like the lads that served to crush you Southern rabble-rousers, Sergeant DuBose. This gang of loafers are in the army because they cannot earn honest livings in the outside world. For them, it is a matter of jail or the barracks," Blackburn said. "You are obviously an educated man, and I don't understand why you have chosen this life. Nor do I care. As far as I am concerned, you are as low-life as they."

Guy's face reddened, but he held his tongue. He tried to keep his mind on the subject of easing up on the men.

"Sir, there is nothing more to be gained by this activity."

"I do not like your attitude, Sergeant DuBose," Blackburn said. "I have felt since my first day in this regiment, that you are a whiner and a troublemaker. Don't try your arrogance on me, or I shall ride you so far down in rank that the horses will consider themselves superior to you."

Guy wisely shut up and went back to his duties. The harsh treatment continued for three more nights. Finally, at reveille on that fourth morning, Blackburn was shocked when 1st Sgt. McClary smugly reported:

"Sir, fourteen men absent."

An initial pursuit was launched, but it brought in only two of the younger fellows who had gotten lost on the trackless prairie. The other twelve were gone for good, and Blackburn was required to report directly to Colonel Gatley to explain the unfortunate situation. After that very unhappy interview, he was forced to call off both his nightly inspections and the continued confinement to the barracks.

Now, relaxing for the first time in a week, Guy and Harry Tate worked steadily at the two bottles of whiskey that Guy had brought with him. Tate, his tongue loosened by the alcohol, gave his friend a long, pensive look. "Guy, I want to say something. But I don't want you to take no offense."

Guy, enjoying his own whiskey-laced coffee, looked over at him.

Harry took a deep breath. "You ought to be an officer, Guy, and that's a fact."

"My service in the Lost Cause prohibits commissioned service," Guy said.

"Then, by damn, if you ain't gonna be one, you shouldn't be in the army."

"I like being a soldier," Guy said.

But Harry wasn't convinced. "Say, don't take this wrong, but you ain't like the rest of us, Guy," he said indicating the other N.C.O.s lounging outside their modest quarters. "I ain't saying you don't fit in, 'cause you do. You got ever'body's respect and the fellers like to have a drink or two with you over to the sutler's store." He paused thoughtfully. "I think the best way to it is to say that if we was on the outside, I'd be working for you, Guy. I'd call you 'Mr. DuBose' like my missus does, and we wouldn't have nothing to do with each other in the social sense."

Martha Tate nodded her agreement. "Why you'd never come to our house to take supper, Mr. DuBose."

Guy knew they were right. But he also knew they would never fully comprehend the reasons for his choice of life in the army. He only shook his head. "You're all wrong."

"No he ain't," Martha Tate said. "And I'd be doing the wash for you just the same."

Harry continued. "As for me, I'm a natural borned enlisted soljer. I'll do anything an officer or that Yankee bastard Blackburn tells me to do. It suits me to make myself the foreman. It's in my nature. I might have thunk the cap'n was wrong as hell, but I kicked them boys up onto them damn rain barrels, and I kicked 'em again when they fell off. I'm a goddamned perfessional soljer—a sergeant—by God I'll do the boss man's bidding. If I wasn't kicking asses here, I'd be doing it out on a plantation work gang."

Martha Tate's voice carried the tone of her conviction. "Mr. DuBose, *you're* a boss man."

"Now wait a minute, both of you," Guy said, a little angry and extremely embarrassed. The conversation was bringing home the unhappy situation in which the war had placed him. "Harry and I have the same job. We work together at it. I am no better than you. I enjoy being invited here to eat, and I value your—"

The urgent notes of *To Arms* sounded from the parade ground.

"Holy Jesus!" Harry yelled. "It's damned near dark too. Let's go."

The two sergeants, suddenly sobered, leaped up and raced to answer the call. The N.C.O. wives on Soap Suds Row called fearfully to their children, gathering their flocks around them. No one knew why the alarm had been sounded. There was the very real possibility that an Indian attack on Fort Alexander was imminent.

Other soldiers, coming from all directions, joined the throng that was now spilling out of barracks, the sutler's store, and other places on post to form up in company and squadron formations.

Reports were quickly taken. Quite a number of men hadn't responded to the trumpet's summons. The members of the guard not on post were organized under their corporals to go out and seek the absentees.

The colonel, unable to waste time, called for all officers and sergeants to march front-and-center to form up close to him.

"I have just received an official report from Mr. Palmer Druce at the Red River Agency that the war chief Lame Elk has left the area and taken a half dozen warriors with him. While seven hostiles does not constitute a great threat, there is always the danger that the longer he remains at liberty, the more followers he will gain. Therefore, it goes without saying, that it is of the utmost importance to pursue and capture him. Lame Elk and his men must be brought back."

The veteran Indian fighters among the troops relaxed a bit then. Only the rookies—and Capt. Gordon Blackburn—remained excited.

The colonel continued. "Every officer, non-commissioned officer, and soldier of the regiment will be fully armed and draw the standard field issue of rations and ammunition. All garrison prisoners will be released as quickly as possible. Third Squadron will remain on post under full alert. I want them ready to take to the field at the shortest notice. Second Squadron will go immediately to the agency and stand by for any necessary action there. First Squadron, with the exception of Company C, will mount patrols that will remain within a five mile radius of the post. Company C will begin an immediate pursuit of Lame Elk and his six men. I want all squadron and troop commanders to report to me at headquarters for further instruction. Remaining officers and N.C.O.s will prepare the men for the coming activities. You are dismissed!"

Guy DuBose and Harry Tate turned immediately to tend to the things they had to do. C Company's men, still disgruntled over the bad treatment, would have been harder to manage, but the prospect of again getting out of garrison raised their collective mood to a higher level. They quickly changed into their field uniforms, then answered *Boots and Saddles*. By the time Captain Blackburn had changed his own clothes and returned to the company, all were ready to ride out.

But Blackburn was not pleased. The picture he saw was not what he'd expected to see. Instead of the men looking like they were ready for another inspection, the troops seemed more as if they were a group of vagrants. Rather than wearing acceptable apparel, all wore old faded, mismatched uniforms. Most had sewn extra patches onto the seats of their trousers to make them last longer and be more comfortable during long hours in the saddle. They sported various types of wide-brimmed headgear which were obviously civilian. Bandannas, mostly red, fleshed out their most unmilitary appearance. If it hadn't been for their carbines, they wouldn't have looked warlike at all.

To make matters worse, both Guy DuBose and Harry Tate were dressed the same way. Blackburn, on the other hand, was impeccable. Not only was he wearing creased trousers and a freshly pressed tunic, but he sported a kepi and even had his saber attached to his well-shined pistol belt. He almost trembled with anger. "DuBose! Come here!" he hissed.

Guy walked up and saluted. "Yes, sir. The company is present and accounted for."

"I won't argue *that* point," Blackburn snapped. "But I will let you know that I do not consider the company properly assembled."

Puzzled, Guy looked around. The outfit, standing motionless and steady, was locked into a precise formation of two sections. Guy turned back to the commanding officer. "I perceive nothing improper, sir."

"Neither you nor Sergeant Tate nor any of the men

are dressed according to regulation, Sergeant," Blackburn said. "Have you not noticed my own uniform?"

"Well, yes, sir," Guy conceded. "But I had thought it was because your previous service did not provide you with old uniforms for field duty. Naturally, you also hadn't had the chance to make any purchases of hats or bandannas at the sutler's store. And I was most respectfully going to remind you that carrying a saber is both unnecessary and unwise in Indian warfare."

"We will discuss all this later, Sergeant," Blackburn said coldly. "Much to your disadvantage and distress, I might add." He motioned to the company. "Let's mount up and get on with our business, Sergeant."

"Yes, sir."

Guy shouted the necessary commands, and the men responded. Within a few moments, C Company, with its brand-new, creased-and-shined proper commanding officer at the front, cantered out of Fort Alexander toward the growing sunset. The guard at the front gate presented arms as the unit rode past.

A lance corporal watched them gallop out into the vast prairie. "By Gott," he said in a thick German accent. "You'd t'ink dat officer vas in front of *der Kaiser* parading."

His companions, two American-born privates, frowned at his butchery of their native language, but one agreed. "Yeah. Cap'n Blackburn is riding out after one of the meanest damn Comanche war chiefs looking like he's about to make *Church Call.*"

The other trooper laughed. "If ol' Lame Elk doubles back and hits them boys, Blackburn'll already be dressed up for his coffin."

CHAPTER 9

Pvt. Tim Donovan, acting as the company scout, walked his horse. Although born in Ireland, he had served nine years in the British Army's campaigns in India. There, battling on the Northwest Frontier side-by-side with the famous Ghurkas, he developed tracking skills that would match any Sioux, Comanche, or Kiowa warrior.

The Irishman was bent over almost double as he studied the tracks on the ground in the rapidly fading sunlight. Blackburn, with Guy slightly behind him, rode up and reined in their horses. The officer made no effort to hide the impatience in his voice. "Can't you move any faster, Private Donovan?"

Donovan, startled, nearly leaped into the position of attention. "Sure, now, sir, and I can."

"Then hop to it, God damn it!" Blackburn snapped.

"Yes, sir." Donovan hesitated. "I beg your pardon, sir. But if I do move faster, I'm afraid that I won't be able to read the spore left by Lame Elk and his band. There ain't a lotta light, sir. What there is won't last."

"Then, Donovan," Blackburn fumed. "That answers the question. It would be pretty stupid to speed up, wouldn't it?"

"Ah, yes, sir," Donovan answered not quite understanding where the conversation was going. He paused for a moment. "Shall I go faster or slower, sir?"

Blackburn gritted his teeth in anger. But before his frazzled temper could explode, Guy DuBose spoke up. "As Private Donovan pointed out, sir, it is getting dark. May I suggest we bivouac for the night and continue the pursuit in the morning?"

"We will not! This patrol has been out hardly two hours," Blackburn said. "Later, there will be a full moon to give us plenty of light."

"Yes, sir," Guy agreed. "But Lame Elk knows he is being chased. The light will also be helpful to him if he decides to spring an ambush on us."

"I would welcome such an unwise action on his part, Sergeant," Blackburn said. "There is only himself with six more miserable savages."

"That was how many left the agency," DuBose reminded him. "Of course this whole episode may just be a tactic of his to goad or tease us. On the other hand, there is a chance he might have been joined by warriors from other Comanche bands or even the Kiowas."

Blackburn became thoughtful.

Guy continued. "Once he perceives we are not continuing after him, he will also camp. In the morning the situation will be the same as it is now."

"Very well," Blackburn conceded. "Have the men dismount and pitch tents."

Guy shook his head. "Captain, we do not travel with tents on patrols like this. They are cumbersome and unnecessary in this weather. The men use bedrolls."

Blackburn frowned. "Is there some plot to make the performance of my duties as difficult as possible?"

"There is not much politicking in a frontier cavalry regiment, sir," Guy said pointedly.

"You know, I am growing more and more disenchanted with your subtle contradictions, Sergeant."

"Yes, sir."

"But, have it your way. I suppose it really makes no difference whether we have a proper military bivouac or not, particularly since the men have the appearance of highway robbers." He paused and gave Guy a meaningful look. "I'm still the new boy, but this constant contradictory attitude of yours will be taken care of as I gain more experience."

"Yes, sir," Guy said. He gestured at Donovan. "Get back to the section."

"Yes, Sargint!"

The company was quickly organized under Guy and Tate's supervision. Pickets were posted and permission was granted to eat cold rations. Guy wanted no fires to attract any wandering marauders during the night. As they settled into the routine, he went to Blackburn's campsite. Guy offered a bandanna. "I always carry an extra, sir."

"I don't want the God damned thing, Sergeant," Blackburn said. "What makes you think I desire to appear as a bandit?"

"Your neck is badly sunburned, sir," Guy said. "Even the late afternoon sun combined with the wind can do damage to exposed skin. It will be worse tomorrow during the brightest hours."

Blackburn instinctively reached back to feel. He

winced as his hand touched the punished skin. He ignored the pain. "Is there at least a cook tent?"

"No, sir," Guy answered. "On small patrols, everyone—officers included—prepares his own food. Hardtack and salt pork. We won't have coffee, only water from canteens."

Blackburn sighed angrily. "Another stupid custom I was not made aware of. I don't suppose anyone drew rations for me."

"Yes, sir," Guy said. "It is customary for the senior N.C.O. to see that the officers' food is included. Trumpeter Pullini will be over directly with yours."

"Very well. You are dismissed, Sergeant."

"Yes, sir." Guy saluted, returning to his camp duties.

The long night was a restless one for Blackburn. He slept only intermittently. The discomfort of lying on the ground was something he could not ignore. After fifteen years of staff duties, he was physically soft. Only his determination and drive kept him in the saddle long after near unbearable fatigue had settled in. The rest he so badly needed was impossible as each toss and turn brought him into contact with rocks, bumps in the ground, and his own equipment—particularly the saber he had laid out beside him.

But by the time Guy and Tate were getting the men out of their bedrolls during the cool pre-dawn hours, Blackburn had just managed to drift off into a deep sleep.

Guy, not wanting the captain to be embarrassed, knelt down beside his slumbering form and roughly shook him. "Captain! Captain!"

Blackburn's eyes opened and he perceived the sergeant through a fatigue-laden haze in the darkness.

"Can't you handle anything alone, Sergeant? Anything that's bothering you can wait until morning."

"Sir," Guy said. "It *is* morning."

By then Blackburn's eyes had opened wide. He could see the men rolling up their gear and preparing for the day. "Of course it is," the officer said forcing himself up. "Anyone can see that." He stood up. "Get someone to roll up my equipment and prepare my horse."

"The horse is ready, sir," Guy said. He turned to the men. "Private Horn! Trumpeter Pullini! You two prepare the captain's gear."

The two young soldiers ran over and set to the task while Blackburn sat on his saddle and pulled on his boots. Guy could tell what was bothering the officer. "Sir, we can heat up some coffee after daylight. It is not wise to light a fire before sunup."

Blackburn felt insulted. "I am not worried over creature comforts, Sergeant. By God, we'll chase those God damned Indians clear to hell and back before we have coffee, understood?"

"Yes, sir."

Blackburn, now fully dressed except for his accouterments, buckled on his belt. "As soon as we're ready, let's get back to the pursuit."

Fifteen minutes later, with bellies trying to digest solid chunks of hardtack and rock-like salt pork, Company C was again on the move after the hostiles.

That morning was a repeat of the previous evening. The hours edged slowly by while Pvt. Tim Donovan, moving slowly and methodically, followed the faint traces left by the fleeing Indians. More dreary time passed uneventfully until they stumbled on a warrior named Young Buffalo. The Indian, an old friend and companion of Lame Elk's, was seated on the ground beside what was an obviously lame horse. He watched dispassionately as the soldiers, with carbines at the ready, approached him.

Young Buffalo raised his hand to Guy DuBose. "Hello, Rides-All-Day."

"Hello, Young Buffalo. What happened to you?" Guy asked.

"My horse no good," Young Buffalo said. "After him rest, I take him back to eat."

Blackburn, who had also arrived on the scene, pointed to the Indian. "And who is that fine fellow?"

"His name is Young Buffalo," Guy explained. "He's one of Lame Elk's closest friends."

Blackburn spat. "Ask him where his closest friend is."

Guy looked down at the calm Indian. "Where did Lame Elk go?"

"Back to agency," Young Buffalo said. He laughed. "He make pony soldier go for a long ride for nothing. No warpath. Just a ride in buffalo country."

"So you think that is funny, do you?" Blackburn asked.

"Sure," Young Buffalo said. "It God damned plenty good funny."

Blackburn pointed to Donovan and young Private Horn. "You two! Get a good grip on that ruffian's wrists and haul him to his feet."

They quickly obeyed. Young Buffalo, his face still impassive, simply stood there waiting to see what was going to happen.

Blackburn tossed his riding quirt to Sgt. Harry Tate who stood near by. "Give him a dozen solid ones."

"Sir?" Harry asked puzzled.

"I want you to lay a dozen lashes on his back," Blackburn said. "You do it with vigor, by God."

Guy DuBose was alarmed. "I beg your pardon, sir."

"Yes, Sergeant?" Blackburn said. "Is there something you wish to say?"

"Sir, I respectfully wish to state—"

"Keep your counsel to yourself," Blackburn said. He nodded toward Harry. "Obey my orders!"

"Yes, sir!"

Harry, not hesitating, walked around to the back of the Comanche. He swung his arm hard, making the quirt whistle through the air. It landed with a resounding whack on the Indian's bare back.

Young Buffalo didn't flinch.

Whack!

The Chogola warrior remained silent.

Ten more blows were delivered with the same result. Blackburn, enraged by the indifference displayed by Young Buffalo, drew his revolver and pointed it straight at the Indian.

Guy shouted, "For the love of God, Captain!"

Blackburn's face reddened with rage. "You will make no statements or utterances unless I call on you to do so, Sergeant DuBose." He swung his hateful gaze back to the Chogola. "What do you think of this, you heathen bastard?"

Young Buffalo said, "I think it a good day to die, you sumbitch."

Blackburn left the muzzle trained on the warrior for several more moments, then he slowly swung the pistol toward the horse. He pulled the trigger. The pistol blasted, and the bullet struck true. The animal wheeled its head one way then the other. Blood gushed from its mouth as it shuddered. The mortally wounded stallion collapsed to its knees, fighting to regain its footing. After a weak whinny, it rolled over on its side and died.

Young Buffalo finally became emotional. "Hey! I want to eat that horse!"

Blackburn, now pleased, yelled over at Donovan. "Study the tracks. Determine if the others really did head back toward the agency."

"Yes, sir." He let go of Young Buffalo's wrist. He didn't have to go far before he found the trail left by the other Indians. "It'll take me a few minutes, sir," he called back.

Blackburn smiled at Young Buffalo, but he spoke to Harry Tate. "Tie his hands."

Harry, not wasting time, reached out and grabbed Young Buffalo by the braids hanging down his back. He jerked hard, pulling the man off balance. Private Horn's grip on the Indian's was broken, and he stepped away.

Harry kicked Young Buffalo's legs, forcing him to the ground. The sergeant knelt down on the Comanche, holding him fast. "Bring me the picket rope off my mount."

Private Horn, glad he was free of the Indian, rushed to obey. "Here you go, Sarge," he said on returning.

"Make it tight," Blackburn said. "I want the bastard to be in pain. Understand? Pain! He'll learn that's what is to be gained by laughing at the United States Army, by God!"

"Yes, sir." Harry obeyed the orders to the letter, cinching the rope up tight. When he was finished he pulled Young Buffalo to his feet.

If the Indian felt any discomfort at all he didn't show it. In fact, he seemed to be quite disinterested in the proceedings. Donovan returned, reporting in with a salute. "Sir, sure and the darlin' heathens is on their way back to the agency."

"Fine," Blackburn said. "Now let's all of us follow after them to make sure." He pointed to Young Buffalo. "Tie that 'darling heathen' to your saddlehorn with a length of rope, Sergeant Tate. If he stumbles or hesitates, encourage him with a good hard jerk."

"Yes, sir."

The small column, with their silent prisoner, formed up and began the trek back to the Red River Agency. They traveled for two hours before Blackburn signaled a halt. "By God," he exclaimed. "Look at that sun, Sergeant DuBose. It's high and hot, is it not?"

"It is, sir."

"Why, Sergeant, you said it would be safe to have a fire after daylight, did you not? I suggest that some strong, hot coffee be brewed up before another minute passes."

Guy glanced back at Young Buffalo. He stood stoically behind Harry Tate's horse. "Shall we untie the prisoner and give him a chance to renew the circulation in his arms, sir?"

"No."

"Yes, sir. May I suggest we loosen the bonds a bit?" Guy persisted.

"You may not."

"Sir—"

"You weary me, Sergeant," Blackburn said. "Dismount the company and let them refresh themselves with hot coffee."

"Yes, sir."

The soldiers wasted no time in starting several fires. Life in the army centered around three things: food, alcohol, and coffee. They had sorely missed their usual hot brew that morning. Within a few minutes they gingerly sipped the liquid from their tin cups. A few of the veterans, wise enough to always plan ahead, even had an extra piece of hardtack to soak in the drink.

Guy DuBose also ingested his share of caffeine stimulation, but he did not enjoy it much. He kept casting glances at Young Buffalo. The Chogola squatted on his haunches, as indifferent to the tight restraints as he was to the cavalry troopers around him.

The rest period went on for over an hour before Captain Blackburn finally ordered the patrol to break the impromptu period of relaxation. They remounted and continued the journey on to the agency.

Another two hours of steady riding brought them across the Red River and into Indian Territory. Their arrival, as Guy DuBose and the other seasoned troopers knew, would be no surprise to the Chogolas. Several warriors on horseback watched them pass by.

Blackburn, at the head of the column, turned and smiled in a superior manner back at Guy. "Well, Sergeant, I think the unexpected sight of this bound prisoner will put fear into those savages."

"I doubt it, sir," Guy said. "They've been trailing us since mid-morning. I'm sure a rider has already gone ahead to tell the tribe of Young Buffalo's treatment."

Blackburn sputtered in anger. "I should have been informed of this, Sergeant DuBose." He shouted to Harry Tate. "Sergeant! Come here on the double!"

Harry, disregarding his prisoner's safety and comfort, slapped his horse into a canter, forcing the Indian to trot behind him. He drew up sharply in front of Blackburn. "Yes, sir?"

"Are you aware that we have been trailed by Indians since this morning?" Blackburn asked.

"Yes, sir," Tate answered. "They been staying on the west side o' the column."

"For the love of God!" Blackburn shouted. "Are you two N.C.O.s complete idiots? Don't you think I should have been made aware of the situation?"

"Jesus, sir!" Harry said. "I thought you knew."

"We could have been attacked."

"No, sir," Guy responded. "When they made no moves right away, we knew they wouldn't. I had the men ready."

Now Blackburn's face was as crimson as his burned neck. "I'll have you court-martialed for this, Sergeant DuBose!"

Guy said nothing.

The column continued on the short distance remaining. When they rode into the agency yard, Palmer Druce rushed forward. His face reflected the alarm he felt. "For the loving mercy of God! Release Young Buffalo!"

Guy looked up and saw that every man in the Chogola tribe, including those who were not followers of Lame Elk, were armed and formed into a semicircle. "I thought the Second Squadron was supposed to be here."

"They left early this morning, Sergeant DuBose," Druce wailed.

Guy reached over and quickly pulled Blackburn's

saber from its scabbard. Guy whirled his horse around and galloped back to where Tate and the prisoner now stood. He swung the weapon, cutting through the rope that ran between the prisoner and Tate. Young Buffalo now came to life. Whooping loudly, he ran to his fellow tribesmen, his arms still bound.

Guy returned the saber to Blackburn. "By your leave, sir."

Before Blackburn could say anything, Palmer Druce spoke his gratitude. "You saved all our lives, Sergeant DuBose. An instant more and every one of those Indians would have fired at us."

The Chogolas, grumbling among themselves, made a slow withdrawal from the scene. Finally all were headed back toward their lodges.

Now Netta Druce came out of the agency store. She was pale and shaken. "I am so glad that is over," she said in a weak voice. The woman fully realized how close she came to being killed by the Indians.

"They have been gathering around here since the rider came back with the news that Young Buffalo was a prisoner," Druce said. "A couple of the warriors even came into the store and openly stole a couple of blankets."

"Do you know them?" Blackburn snapped. "We shall hunt them out and bring the thieves to a quick brand of justice."

"Oh, Captain, please!" Netta cried out. She looked at Guy DuBose, her eyes boldly looking deep into his for the first time. "Don't let him do anything, Sergeant DuBose."

Druce reached up and grabbed Blackburn's arm. "If you go into the Chogola camp none of us will see this

108

day's sunset."

Blackburn sneered. "Dramatic words, but they do not impress a soldier."

"I am impressed," Guy said.

Blackburn, fully realizing he was a newcomer to this sort of situation, decided to calm down. But he wasn't going to end on a whimpering note. "I'll be back," he vowed. "And this will be the last time that I shall hesitate to take direct action against any of those savages!" He jerked his head around to face Guy. "We'll return to Fort Alexander and I'll report in to Colonel Gatley."

"You mustn't go," Mrs. Druce said close to tears. "The Indians might come back."

Guy took charge. "Trumpeter Pullini, ride back to the post and inform the regimental sergeant major of the situation here."

"Yes, Sergeant!" Pullini yelled from the column. He immediately galloped out of the formation and turned southward.

Blackburn sputtered. "I'll give—where is he— Trumpeter! Trumpeter! Return immediately!"

But it was too late. The young soldier was already going hell for leather in the direction of the Red River. Blackburn whipped around to DuBose, his dark eyes flashing the rage the officer felt toward the sergeant.

CHAPTER 10

Colonel Gatley drummed his fingers on the desk, glaring across its battered expanse at Capt. Gordon Blackburn.

"So you have stepped forward and brought charges against Sergeant DuBose?" the colonel asked.

"I most certainly have, sir," Blackburn answered. "The papers have been properly drawn up per court-martial procedures as directed in army regulations. I have turned them into the adjutant for filing."

"I am certain they have," Gatley said. "You have a plethora of experience in administrative matters, have you not?"

"I have, sir."

"You are aware, of course, that such action requires an investigation," Colonel Gatley said.

"I certainly am."

"A complete record of the accused's service must also be included," Gatley continued. "That would encompass his dates of enlistment, statement of character, record of promotions, and other information."

"I have done that, sir," Blackburn said confidently.

"And where are these documents, Captain?"

"Sir, they, like the charges I've brought against the sergeant, are with the regimental adjutant," Blackburn answered.

"Sergeant DuBose is one of the most valued non-commissioned officers in this regiment," Colonel Gatley said.

"That surprises me, sir," Blackburn said in a feigned hurt tone. "Especially after my sad experience with him."

Gatley, feeling fretful and worried, lit his pipe. He smoked for several minutes before going on. "As a matter of fact, Captain, there is no doubt in my mind that our man DuBose will someday be the regimental sergeant major."

"Not if he is broken down and kept a private soldier as he should be," Blackburn insisted.

The colonel decided against rushing into the situation. Blackburn made him nervous. This sudden appearance from the War Department in apparent disgrace did not mean that the man was totally without influential friends in the army. The captain might still have a few cards yet to play in the political games of the higher echelons. "I understand that you became agitated with the men's appearance prior to going on patrol."

Blackburn thought fast. "Yes, sir. That was due to my inexperience, I confess. Though, in my defense, I will point out that certain customs and practices have not been revealed to me by the N.C.O.s in my company. Neither have I been helped much, I am afraid to report, by my fellow officers. I was no more

112

aware of the permitted relaxation of uniform regulations during duty in the field, than I was of the fact that brevet ranks are not recognized in this regiment."

Gatley nodded. "I understand from my officers, Captain, that you are a difficult man to get to know," he said diplomatically. "I must also say that unnecessarily ranking the Robertsons out of quarters did little to gain you any of their affection or trust."

"What I insisted on were my rights according to regulations," Blackburn said.

"It was not wise of you, nevertheless, Captain."

"Whatever the reason I have not been made welcome," Blackburn said.

"I believe the Robertsons have made you a permanent dinner guest until your wife's arrival," Gatley pointed out. "I think that was very generous of them under the circumstances."

"Only proper courtesy," Blackburn insisted.

"Well, the unhappy situation between you and the other officers must be alleviated as quickly as possible," Gatley said. "But let us go back to our discussion of Sergeant DuBose. What are the specifics of your objections to his conduct? And why is the situation so bad that you feel a court-martial is necessary?"

"First of all, sir, I blame him entirely for the appalling number of desertions in Company C," Blackburn said.

Now Gatley didn't give a damn about any political infighting from the captain. He leaned forward, his voice louder, "God damn it, Captain! I believe that the episode of confinement and nightly inspections you insisted on conducting spurred that unhappy situation."

"That is debatable, Colonel," Blackburn said. "But there are a few areas of Sergeant DuBose's conduct that will support no argument whatsoever. He was insolent during the entire patrol, going out of his way to contradict me and make my office as commander in the field as difficult as possible. All of this was done within sight and hearing of the lower-ranking enlisted men."

"Perhaps, Captain," Gatley said now calmed down. "You misread his attempts to advise you as an argumentative attitude on the sergeant's part."

"Why did he not tell me of the Indians who were following our column?" Blackburn asked. "If he was so aware of my need for counsel, why did he not take pains to see that I was aware of that dangerous situation?"

"That could be construed as a shortcoming," Gatley conceded. "But it can also be assumed that he thought you knew they were out there."

"He freed a prisoner of war without proper authorization," Blackburn said, feeling his position weakening considerably.

Now Gatley pounced. "That was an absolutely correct course of action, Captain Blackburn. If he hadn't cut that warrior loose immediately, you would have had an overwhelming number of Chogolas sweep over your command. You all, including the Druces, would have been murdered within minutes."

Blackburn seethed inside, but kept quiet.

"We are going to have a war this summer, Captain," Gatley said. "There is no doubt about that. There is every indication that it will be impossible to keep the Chogola Comanches pinned inside the agency. Even

114

Palmer Druce, as devoted a pacifist Christian as ever came down the pike, admits that Lame Elk is going to gather up a large band of fighting males to raid down in Texas. Active campaigning is a certainty. Sergeant DuBose participated in some of the fiercest fighting in which the regiment was involved. He proved his valor and qualities of leadership during the action."

"I do not approve of him," Blackburn said doggedly.

Gatley bore in. "I would feel much better if an experienced battle leader such as Sgt. Guy DuBose was in a position of leadership. Wouldn't you, Captain? Now tell me the absolute truth as gentleman to gentleman."

Blackburn knew that he was being offered an honorable way out. He had drawn up the charges. If it appeared that he changed his mind and withdrew them, there would be no damage to his reputation or prestige as an officer.

Gatley didn't want to take any chances. "Lieutenant Harris," he called out to the adjutant. "Please bring in the court-martial papers on Sergeant DuBose."

Harris made an immediate appearance. He handed the documents to Gatley who, in turn, slid them across the desk to Blackburn. The colonel smiled in a fatherly way. "Have you made up your mind yet, Captain?"

Blackburn hesitated, then he grabbed the papers. He methodically ripped them in half. "I think it wise that I give Sergeant DuBose another chance, sir. I must think of the regiment, mustn't I?"

"Yes you must," the colonel said still smiling. He reached over and pulled the ripped legal drafts back to his side of the desk. After dropping them in the waste basket, he asked, "Was there anything else you needed, Captain?"

Blackburn stood up. "No, sir. Thank you, sir." After a quick salute he made his exit, walking through the adjutant's office and out the building.

Gordon Blackburn hated to lose. And he had just lost big. After going to a lot of trouble to break DuBose down, he'd been turned aside and twisted to the extent that he, himself, had been forced to call off the court-martial. When he arrived back at C Company's orderly room, he was in a foul mood. "Sergeant McClary!" he bellowed as he entered.

McClary, who had been working on the company sick report book, looked up, then scrambled to his feet. "Yes, sir!"

"Fetch Sergeant DuBose here immediately," Blackburn hissed through clenched teeth. "And make yourself scarce until I am finished with him."

"Yes, sir!"

The first sergeant rushed off to tend to the errand. Blackburn sat down at his desk. He glanced around the primitive room that served as the headquarters of Company C. Back in the War Department he'd had an office to himself that was more than three times the size of that orderly room. Not only had it been filled with high quality furniture, but two men—a corporal and a civilian clerk—were assigned to him to process the paper that flowed through the administrative mill.

Five minutes passed before Sgt. Guy DuBose made his appearance. He knocked on the door, removed his kepi, and entered. "Sir, Sergeant DuBose reporting to the company commander as ordered."

Blackburn returned the salute. "Stand at ease." He lit a cigar, glaring at the N.C.O. during the process.

116

"You have a lot of friends in this regiment, Sergeant."

"Yes, sir," Guy answered a bit puzzled.

"I don't mean your fellow sergeants," Blackburn said. "I am referring particularly to headquarters and the colonel."

Guy said nothing.

Blackburn continued. "I will be perfectly candid with you. They saved you from a court-martial. Oh, the charges were impressive." He counted them off on his fingers. "Let's see. There was conduct unbecoming a non-commissioned officer, disrespect to a commissioned officer, refusal to obey orders, misconduct in the face of the enemy, and even sedition."

Guy remained silent.

"But your good friend Colonel Gatley squelched this exercise in military justice, Sergeant," Blackburn said. "Aren't you happy about that? Answer me!"

"Yes, sir," Guy said.

"You know, Sergeant, I am well aware that every member of this regiment, from the colonel commanding right down to lowest-ranking garrison prisoner, is aware that my transfer here was a result of political infighting in the War Department," Blackburn said. "Frankly, I couldn't care less what the scum think. Do you know why?"

"No, sir."

"Because, like you, I have friends," Blackburn said. "This set-back in my military career is only temporary, believe me. It is only a matter of time before I'll be back in Washington City, and you can bet there'll be a pair of maple leafs on my shoulder straps to boot. I have contacts not only inside but outside the army that will set things right for me." He began to smoke thoughtfully. "A quick run through lieutenant colonel and colonel should take perhaps two years before I'm a brigadier general. When that happens, I shall get my revenge on certain individuals who crossed me."

"Yes, sir."

"Oh, not you, Sergeant DuBose," Blackburn said. "You are just small fry. By that time you will be no more than a minor bad memory. Like the flies and growing heat of this accursed post."

"Yes, sir," Guy replied. "Perhaps it would be best for everyone concerned if I transferred to another company."

Blackburn shook his head. "No, Sergeant. I want you around for amusement. You are going to become my personal errand boy. What do you think of that?"

"I have always performed my duty, sir."

"How admirable, Sergeant," Blackburn said. "You will have an opportunity to prove your devotion. My wife is due in on the train at Dahlquart tomorrow. I want you to form up an escort and take the ambulance to meet her."

"Yes, sir," Guy said. "In cases like this, it is customary for another lady to go along, sir. Mrs. Tate has always been available to act as a temporary companion to incoming officers' wives. Sometimes the discomforts of this part of the country can best be softened by another woman's presence."

"An excellent idea, Sergeant," Blackburn said. "I'll leave the arrangements to you. Just see that you serve my wife as well as any house servant should. Dismissed!"

Guy saluted. He stepped back outside into the fresh air. He could see McClary standing down by D

118

Company's orderly room talking with their first sergeant. Guy walked down to them. "You can go back now."

"Jesus, DuBose," McClary said. "You're in trouble with the captain."

"Not really," Guy joked. "He's asked me to fetch his wife at Dahlquart tomorrow."

D Company's first sergeant, a big Scot named Sinclair, laughed. "I'll warrant ye, ye'll find a real bitch there, DuBose. Why else would he have *you* get her, hey? He's probably scared to death of her himself."

"Yeah," McClary laughed. "What kind of a woman would marry a devil like Blackburn?"

"I'm not worried," Guy said with a grin. "Martha Tate will be there to protect me."

"How many men are you taking?" McClary asked. He was always worried about the condition of his duty roster.

"Lame Elk is going to be resting up for awhile," Guy replied. "I don't think I'll need more than three."

"Get 'em outta your section," McClary said. "Most o' Tate's men are slated for regimental guard with him tomorrow."

"Right," Guy said. "I'll leave Corporal Hansen in charge of the men left behind." He walked away. "I'm going back to drill."

The two N.C.O.s watched him leave. "There's two bad things are gonna happen this summer, Sergeant Sinclair," McClary said.

"What might they be, Sergeant McClary?"

"The first is an Injun war and the second is either Blackburn or DuBose being murdered by the other."

CHAPTER 11

Dahlquart, Texas was a small town that made up for its lack of size with boisterous noise, unceasing activity, and murderous violence. Senseless killings on the main street between drunken, enraged frontiersmen were such frequent happenings that they hardly drew any attention. Colonel Gatley was perfectly content in the knowledge that the wild community was too far away from Fort Alexander to offer its saloons and whorehouses to his troops.

Although known officially as a railhead, the town was more of a rail's end. The tracks coming down from Missouri and across Louisiana ran straight across the greater center of Texas and ended abruptly at Dahlquart in the west. The town grew up around that termination of steel rails and wooden ties.

The rail accommodations offered were not enough to distract the great cattle drives from their moves north into Kansas. The train services at Dodge City and Wichita were much more superior. But Dahlquart did serve as as convenient gathering and meeting place for people wishing to conduct business-legal and otherwise—in northwest Texas.

The appearance of an army ambulance carrying a driver and woman and escorted by four mounted soldiers attracted no more than cursory glances from the loafers, working folks, and visitors on the street. Most of these looks were decidedly unfriendly. The respect the civilian population—even the lowest drifters—had for the soldiery depended on the extent of hostile Indian activity. The more raids, the more regard. Most of the time a trooper got no more than snubs or insults. But when the Kiowas and Comanches kicked up their heels, there was nothing good enough for the boys sporting army blue.

Sgt. Guy DuBose, leading the small group, turned in his saddle and motioned the driver to head toward the railroad depot. The teamster clicked his tongue at the mule and pulled on the reins. Martha Tate, sitting beside him, hollered over to Guy. "It 'pears the train has already come, Mr. DuBose." She pointed to the stack of freight and other unclaimed goods on the platform.

"So it does, Mrs. Tate," Guy responded. He rode on a bit faster with Privates Tim Donovan, Ben Horn, and Paddy McNally sticking close behind him. When they arrived at the depot, all dismounted. Guy called the soldiers over to him. "Remember we're here on official business, so stay right here by the horses," he said. He gave a particularly meaningful look to Donovan. "I'll have none of you going to a saloon. Is that understood?"

"Sure and it is, Sargint," Donovan replied. "As a

member of the Good Templars, I'd not do such a thing."

McNally laughed. "Now there's malarkey if I ever heard it."

Donovan growled, "Is it a liar you're callin' me, Private McNally?"

"Oh, no, Private Donovan," McNally replied with a challenging grin. "It's just that I've no faith in yer nature."

"Then that shows how little ye know me, Private McNally."

McNally shook his head. "By all that's holy in the auld sod, ye're an Irishman. It just ain't a natural thing fer ye not to drink."

"That's enough!" Guy interjected. He wanted no donnybrooks in public between the two Irishmen. "Wait here and stay out of trouble. You can discuss the drinking habits of the Irish race when you're back on post and, preferably, behind the barracks."

"Now I'm thinkin' we'll do just that," Donovan said with a meaningful glare at McNally.

Young Ben Horn, still fearful that Donovan would find out he was the one who bashed him the night the old soldier was arrested, hung back nervously. He found the opposite side of his horse very interesting as he adjusted and re-adjusted the stirrup straps.

When the ambulance joined them, Guy helped Martha Tate step down to the ground. She still seemed fresh despite the four-hour trip. "Now let's go find our little lady , Mr. DuBose. She must be plumb worried what with nobody meeting her." Martha glanced around. "And in a awful place like Dahlquart! It ain't

123

fit for decent folks."

"After you, Mrs. Tate."

They ascended the wooden steps to the station platform. "I'll look outside, you check with the station master," Martha said.

Guy went directly to the barred window and rapped on it. "Mister, did a lady arrive on the last train? We're supposed to meet one of the officers' wives here."

"I think I seen one that fits the bill. She's inside the waiting room," the man answered.

"How long ago did the train arrive?" Guy asked.

"Oh, 'bout two hours I'd say."

"Pretty damned early," Guy said testily. "How the hell did that happen?"

"It didn't happen, soljer boy. It's really about a day late," the man said with a laugh. "The schedule we're on is yesterday's. Dahlquart-bound engines get the last priority outta Shreveport."

Martha Tate joined him. "She ain't out here."

"The waiting room," he answered. Guy led the way toward the door thinking that he should tell the quartermaster that the railroad timetables used at Fort Alexander would have to be considered days, not hours late. The regiment depended on the railroad for needed supplies as well as transport.

Guy and Mrs. Tate stepped into the small waiting area and noticed a woman sitting on the farthest bench. She faced away from them, but her clothing was definitely in the style and expense that bespoke Washington City society.

"Mrs. Blackburn?" he asked.

"Yes," she answered standing up. She turned around, then her eyes opened wide in shocked astonishment. "Oh, dear Lord!"

Guy clenched his teeth hard. For an instant the emotional wave that swept over him threatened to sink him to his knees. Pauline Berger—his Pauline—stood looking at him through the light veil that flowed down from her hat and covered her face.

"Why, child!" Martha exclaimed rushing forward. Pauline had staggered backward, and only the older woman's efforts kept her from falling. "What in the world?"

"I—we—everyone—thought you were dead," Pauline said weakly. She stared as if fascinated beyond reason by Guy's presence. He was older, a bit more rough looking, but as handsome as ever. "It is you, isn't it? You are Guy DuBose!"

"Yes. It's me," Guy answered in a weak voice.

"I never in my wildest hopes and dreams—" She recovered enough from her near lapse into unconsciousness to begin weeping. "Oh, Guy! Oh, Guy!"

Martha tenderly slipped an arm around her and led her back to the bench. "Now you just sit down and recover yourself." She looked at Guy. "What is this all about, Mr. DuBose?"

Guy swallowed hard, then wiped his lips with the back of his hand. "Pauline—that is, Mrs. Blackburn and I were once—we were friends in Charleston."

"You was more than friends, Mr. DuBose!" Martha snapped. "I ain't dumb and blind."

Pauline pulled a handkerchief from her sleeve. She slipped it under the veil and wiped her eyes. "Selby came back and said you'd been killed at Gettysburg."

"Selby's dead," Guy said coldly.

"I know, Guy. He was sent home with the wounded

125

on a parole," Pauline said. "They'd taken off one of his legs. He died at his family's home after only being back a month or so. He said he saw you fall on the last day of the battle."

The emotions of the moment finally overwhelmed Guy. He turned abruptly and stormed outside to the platform. Now everything he'd joined the army for—forgetfulness, solitude, and escape—were shattered beyond repair. The one terrible occurrence in his life that had driven him away had not only caught up with him, but had been flung straight into his face like a slap from the devil himself. His heart broke anew, and his soul wept with fresh tears.

Guy walked up to one of the crates and drove his fist straight into it, making the wood creak and bend with the force. "God damn it!" he whispered furiously. "God damn it! God damn it! God damn it!"

Moments later the two women appeared. Pauline seemed to be under control, and Martha Tate spoke softly but firmly to Guy. "I think it best that we keep this to ourselves, Mr. DuBose. A army post is a terrible small place with lots o' big mouths. Gossip can be hurtful. It won't do nobody no good if folks knowed about you and the lady."

"Of course," Guy agreed.

"I ain't even gonna tell Harry about it," Martha said. "And don't you neither." She smiled encouragement to the woman. "You hear that, dear?"

"Yes—yes—thank you," Pauline replied.

"Now, Mister DuBose, Mrs. Blackburn's luggage is yonder at the edge o' the platform. You'd best get them boys to fetch it."

Guy, saying nothing, walked back to where the

126

troopers and the ambulance waited. "You three!" he snapped. "Get the lady's stuff. It's at the far end of the platform."

"Yes, Sargint!" Donovan answered with enthusiasm. As he ascended the stairs with Horn and McNally at his heels, he tipped his kepi to Pauline. "And the top o' the day to you, Missus."

Pauline smiled weakly and allowed Mrs. Tate to take her down to the ambulance. It took the three men two trips to get all the baggage. Finally, with the entire load on board and strapped down, the ambulance, with escort, was again on the road.

Guy purposely stayed fifteen yards in front of the wagon. The last thing he needed at the moment was contact with Pauline. The two women sat in the back on the bench seats. They talked softly and intimately together as instant feelings of trust and friendship grew between them. Donovan, Horn, and McNally were positioned in a semi-circle covering the rear of the vehicle. They wondered what had soured their sergeant's disposition to such an extent.

The trip continued across the rolling terrain for another two hours. The three troopers and the driver were not sure, but something seemed out of the ordinary to them. Even the lady they'd fetched was out of sorts. Obviously something had happened between her and Sergeant DuBose, but none could figure out what it was. The sergeant had acted downright surly toward them on a couple of occasions when they had made friendly overtures toward him in the guise of jokes and bantering.

Now, properly subdued, the soldiers settled back to see what was going to happen on the trip. Finally,

Martha Tate turned around in her seat and called out loudly to Guy:

"Mr. DuBose! Mr. DuBose!"

Guy ignored her for a few moments, but knew he would have to answer. He reluctantly and slowly wheeled his horse around and allowed the animal to slowly walk back. "Yes, Mrs. Tate?"

"I do think it's time for a rest stop," Martha Tate said sweetly. She indicated a copse of redbud trees.

"Yes, ma'am."

The driver, without waiting to be told, turned the correct direction. He drew up to a stop and hopped down. "I reckon I'll stretch my legs," he said diplomatically as he walked over to join the other soldiers who had drawn off a discreet distance. Guy started to follow them, but Mrs. Tate called to him.

"Please stay by the wagon and help me down, Mr. DuBose."

"Of course." He dismounted and offered his hand.

"I'll be back directly," Martha said. "You wait here."

Guy, feeling awkward, stood in silence beside the ambulance. He fumbled through his pockets for a cigar.

Pauline spoke in a soft voice. "Do you still like those Spanish cheroots, Guy?" The words were casual and friendly, but her voice trembled with barely controlled emotion.

"I can't afford them on sergeant's pay," he said tersely.

"Guy, we must speak," Pauline said. "It is so important to me."

"It wouldn't be proper, ma'am," he replied. "You're an officer's lady and I am an enlisted man."

128

Pauline sighed audibly. "Guy! Please! I have never in my life experienced such overwhelming shock and surprise. I do not see how we can avoid each other. It will be impossible."

He finally looked her straight in the eyes. "Pauline, there is nothing for us to talk about. The past is gone and dead. I would prefer that we leave it that way. Our lives are now on different levels."

Pauline started to speak again but reconsidered. She simply said, "Yes, Guy."

Martha returned. "Mrs. Blackburn?"

Guy, without waiting to be asked, offered his arm. Pauline took it and stepped down. Her touch went to the core of his being like a gently persistent probe of lightning.

Fifteen minutes later the journey to the garrison resumed. The final two hours, like the first, were ridden in strained silence. When they finally went through the gate, Guy broke off to report to Captain Blackburn.

He found him in the orderly room with old Capt. Dan Wayne. Guy saluted. "Sir, your wife has been delivered to your quarters."

"Thank you, Sergeant," Blackburn said. He offered his hand to Wayne. "Good luck to you in your retirement. Now, if you will excuse me, I'll go see my wife. I've not seen her for more than two months now."

Guy felt a pang of jealous hurt. Wayne walked over and patted him on the shoulder. "Well, Sergeant DuBose, I must say goodby to you of all people."

"Goodby, sir. It was an honor serving under your command," Guy said.

Wayne laughed. "The hell it was! I'll not deny my inattention to duty at this point in my life. Because of it, you and Tate had to work harder than any other line sergeants in the regiment. But, at any rate, you are one of the finest non-commissioned officers I have ever known." He paused. "Now get the hell out of the army, DuBose!"

"Sir?"

"You don't belong here, young man. You're stagnating. What's left for you? A sergeant major's post when you're a pot-bellied old drunkard? Or, if you're really unlucky, you'll end up with a court-martial from some son of a bitch like Blackburn?"

"I don't know, sir," Guy said shaking his head.

"There's damned little future for even a commissioned officer," Wayne said. "Because of having served the Rebel cause, you will never wear shoulder straps. And you're not cut out to be an enlisted man."

Guy remembered his conversation with the Tates. "I've heard that before," he admitted.

"When is your hitch up?" Wayne asked.

"I've another eight months," Guy answered.

"I'll tell you what, Sergeant," Wayne said. "I'm going to join my brother in a land business down in Dallas. When I get there I'll send you my new address. Perhaps if you decide not to re-enlist, you would be interested in an offer of a position."

"Thank you, sir."

"I can't promise you anything of course, but perhaps the situation will be to your benefit."

"I appreciate the consideration," Guy said. At that point, after seeing Pauline, even getting out of the army to sweep saloons seemed a blessing.

Wayne offered his hand again. "I hope to see you again, Sergeant. I truly do."

But now Guy wasn't listening. His mind, despite all efforts to stop it, was full of Pauline. She looked only a little older and a bit sadder. But her beauty, as radiant as ever, still pulled at his heartstrings. The mental picture was pleasant, but soon another thought pushed it aside with cruel persistence.

Now he could imagine the agonizing picture of Pauline in the arms of Capt. Gordon Blackburn.

CHAPTER 12

Netta Druce, refreshed from her night's sleep, walked into the kitchen of the home she shared with her husband on the Red River Agency. There was still an early morning chill in the spring air. Netta instinctively pulled the shawl on her shoulders tighter. "Isn't the fire built up yet?" she asked her young Mexican house-keeper Inez.

"No, *Señora,*" she answered. "I am putting the wood in the stove now."

"Mr. Druce will be cranky if his coffee is late," Netta complained.

Inez, a feisty nineteen-year-old, shrugged her in-difference. "There is no water anyway." The young woman had spent three years as a captive of the Chogolas. She'd been virtually unnoticed in the village because of her dark skin coloring, but several soldiers from Fort Alexander had finally become attracted to the pretty girl. They were the ones who found out Inez was Mexican. She had learned to speak a bit of English because of living near the Texas border. A brief conversation alerted them to her true position in the tribe. The troopers wasted no time in informing their company commander of the situation. Consequently, a great effort was launched to free her. When the Indians finally agreed to let Inez go, everyone involved was surprised when Inez strongly expressed her desire to stay at the agency rather than go back to her home village in Mexico.

She had been captured during a bold Comanche raid on a market town in Chihuahua. After being carried off and raped, she was kept as a squaw by a Chogola warrior. Inez knew that these unhappy circumstances, though beyond her control, would make her considered no less than a whore by her own people. Even the young Mexican woman's parents would have had nothing to do with her, and none of the young men would have taken her as a wife. If she did go back to Mexico, there was every chance that she would have eventually been driven into prostitution. At least at the agency she had the opportunity to meet lonely soldiers. With a bit of luck she knew she would eventually be married to one. Washing clothes on Soap Suds Row was preferable to life in a bordello crib.

Netta joined Inez in the morning chores. She liked working in the kitchen. The tasks kept her hands busy and allowed her mind to dwell on other things such as daydreaming about the handsome Sgt. Guy DuBose. Although she'd denied it to herself for many months, Netta finally had to admit that she was profoundly and seriously attracted to the soldier. His good manners, soft manner of speaking, and courtly grace were irresistible to even this devoutly Christian woman.

Her husband Palmer was an impatient, excitable

man. The slightest break in routine or even a small mistake on her part in running the agency store would set him off into hours of scolding and complaining. He constantly monitored her classes with the Indian children and found fault in every lesson she taught. Their evenings were filled with hours of criticism and petulant lectures that drove her to tears. Netta always promised Palmer that she would try harder, but no matter what effort she made, he was never satisfied. She had been brought up to be obedient to her husband, but many times she found this devotion sorely tried.

Sgt. Guy DuBose, on the other hand, was the emotional opposite of Palmer Druce. Quiet and sure of himself, he seemed to move through his martial life with everything under his control. Even when giving orders to his soldiers, he remained remarkably low-keyed and calm. Netta, to her utmost shame, had even wondered what it would be like to be a wife to the sergeant and share his bed.

Several times, Guy DuBose had spoken to her. The manner of his approach had been one of offering friendship and an opportunity to allow whatever association was possible between them to develop to its fullest. Netta, despite her naivete where men were concerned, could recognize the chance for romance. But painful shyness always made her feel stupid and ugly. She knew she was far from beautiful, but on the frontier there was no competition from other women. It was her most secret and most wonderful private thought that if she could overcome her timidness she could have a *liaison d'amour* with Guy DuBose. During periods of anger at Palmer, she enjoyed

135

creating fantasies in her mind in which she and Sergeant DuBose ran off together to live in delightful sin and carnal pleasure.

"Señora," Inez said interrupting her thoughts. "I talked with Two Pony's woman yesterday. She will bring the corn meal today. To make *tortillas.* I promised, remember? You said you wanted to learn."

"What?"

"Ay! You are not listening to me, eh? Where is your mind, *Señora?"* Inez smiled and winked. The Mexican girl had noticed Netta's furtive glances at the *gringo* sergeant. "Do you have a man you think of?"

Netta's anger and guilt quickly boiled to the surface. "Of course not, you stupid girl! What a terrible thing to say!"

Inez, unbothered, shrugged. *"Y que?* What's so wrong with that? A husband can be tiresome while a handsome man is not to be wasted even in one's mind, no?"

The statement came so close to the truth that it made Netta's face flush. "Get back to your work!"

But Inez persisted in her teasing. "Tell me. Who is he?"

Netta faced the girl with a face as hard as granite. "You are accusing me of unchristian behavior!"

"Gringa fria!" Inez said under her breath.

Netta's conscience reacted again when her husband Palmer joined them. "Good morning, ladies," he called out. "Am I in time for a nice cup of fresh coffee?"

Inez, still smiling to herself, remained silent. Netta picked up the wooden bucket and handed it to her husband. "Please, Palmer. We'll need some water for coffee."

"No coffee?" he asked. "Now really, Netta! You know how I like a hot cup when I first arise. You should have had some brewing by first light this morning."

"I didn't think about it," Netta said. "I am sorry, Palmer."

"Sometimes you are very disappointing, Netta," Palmer said in a solemn tone.

"Please, Palmer. Get the water," Netta said.

"This most certainly is not the end of this situation, Netta," Palmer Druce said firmly.

"Inez should have known enough to get water for coffee," Netta said defensively.

"Do not blame her, Netta. You are the mistress of this particular castle," Palmer said. "We shall speak of this later. Meantime, I shall fetch the water." He made a dignified exit from the house.

Inez turned and smiled. "Daydreaming is nice, no? You don't have to tell me, *Señora,* I know who he is. It is the handsome sergeant, no?"

"You wicked, wicked girl! Be quiet!" Netta exclaimed. She gave her full attention to slicing the bacon. She'd barely started when Palmer burst back through the door. He didn't have the bucket.

"Please Lord save us all!" he cried out.

"What is the matter, Palmer?" Netta asked in terror. Inez, fearful, looked at him with her dark eyes opened wide.

"There are missing lodges in the Chogola camp," Palmer said. "I counted them. At least a third are gone. I must hurry to Fort Alexander."

"No, Palmer!" Netta begged. "The Indians will come here and kill us."

But Inez had calmed down. "Do not worry," she said

137

in a relieved tone. "If the lodges are gone, so too is Lame Elk and his warriors. There is no danger at the agency."

Palmer spent no more time in talk. He left the women and rushed to the stable to saddle his horse. Within a few minutes he was galloping through the ford on the Red River, headed directly for the army post.

Druce pounded across the rolling plains country unmindful of prairie dog holes or other dangers to his mount. By the time he reached the fort's main gate, his eyes were wide with growing fear. The guards, recognizing him, did not challenge the visitor. Their attempts to slow him down to find out what was wrong were in vain as he sped past them and wheeled toward regimental headquarters.

The frantic man did not bother to tie his horse at the hitching rail in front of the building. He leaped from the saddle and bounded up the steps, rushing through the door past the startled sergeant major's desk. He bounded into Colonel Gatley's office, then came back out just as fast.

"Where is the colonel, for the love of dear God?" he demanded.

"Calm down, Mr. Druce," Sgt. Maj. Bradley said. "I'll have his orderly fetch him."

The young soldier, just back from eating his breakfast, was seated in a chair by the door picking his teeth. "What's the matter, Mr. Druce?"

"For the love of God!" Palmer yelled. "Go get the colonel!"

The soldier smirked. "Colonel Gatley don't take kindly to being fetched."

The sergeant major exploded. "Get off your butt and get the colonel!"

The orderly leaped up and rushed off to fetch the commanding officer. The sergeant major tried to calm the excited man. "I think you better sit down, Mr. Druce."

"Sit down?" Druce cried. "Lame Elk has taken a full third of the Chogolas with him and fled the agency."

"Shit!" the sergeant major snapped. Then, remembering that Druce was a man of the cloth, he apologized.

But Palmer Druce didn't notice. "Where is he? Where is he?"

"The colonel will get here as quick as he can," Bradley said.

Druce, pacing back and forth, kept glancing out the window. Finally he yelled, "Ah!" and raced to the door, throwing it open. "Colonel Gatley, please hurry!"

The colonel, alarmed, entered the building. He ignored Sergeant Major Bradley's salute. "What the hell is the matter, Mr. Druce?"

"Colonel, Lame Elk has taken a third of the Chogolas with him and left the agency," Druce said.

Gatley sighed. "So it's started, hey?" His voice was calm. "Now we know for sure how we'll spend the summer."

Bradley stepped forward. "Shall I have the duty trumpeter sound *Assembly*, sir?"

"Yes, Sergeant. Immediately, if you please."

"Yes, sir!"

A flurry of activity began around Fort Alexander. The well-drilled regiment formed up quickly to receive their commander's orders. There was no danger to the post or the agency at the moment. The hell that was to roll across Texas was already on its way south, and it was in that unhappy place where the first violence would play out in the drama of that summer.

The First Squadron, with Company C in the vanguard, was the leading unit dispatched to the field. This time, in a newly purchased slouch hat with a broad brim and sporting a fresh, bright bandanna around his neck, Capt. Gordon Blackburn rode at the head of the command with the guidon bearer and Trumpeter Benito Pullini to his immediate rear. Just behind them, leading his section, Sgt. Guy DuBose sat ramrod straight in the saddle, his body moving easily with the cantering of his horse. Behind that section, Sgt. Harry Tate led his own men.

C Company, which by the official organization of the army should have numbered more than sixty, had barely mustered thirty soldiers to answer that morning's trumpet call to action. Understrength units like this one were the result of public apathy and a stingy congress. Sergeants earned $17 a month while corporals were paid $15 and privates $13 to enforce a giddy, inconsistent police toward the unconquered Indians.

This time Private Donovan's expertise in tracking was not needed. With so many women and children, belongings, and the buffalo skin lodges, the Chogolas left an easy trail. The travois and tracks of many moccasins and horses created a twenty-foot wide swath through the grass.

Later, as the spore became fresher, Guy spurred his horse and rode up to the company commander. "Begging your pardon, sir."

"Yes, Sergeant? What is it?"

"I suggest flankers and an advance guard, if you please," Guy said. "We're drawing closer to the hostiles. They may spring an ambush to give their families a chance to break loose and gain more distance from us."

"I'll leave that to you, Sergeant," Blackburn said wisely.

"Yes, sir." Guy sent some of his own men forward while Tate donated three to each side of the column. These outriders, all good soldiers with excellent eyesight, kept a constant vigil on likely spots from which attacks could be sprung up close. They also scanned the horizon for the sight of the Chogola's version of a full-mounted charge.

The pursuit continued more slowly and with more care. After three long hours a smudge of smoke was sighted on the horizon. Blackburn was delighted. "Sergeant DuBose! Front and center!"

Guy rode up to the officer. "Yes, sir?"

"Is that an Indian signal fire? I've read about such things back east. Perhaps it's a message to attack the column."

Guy shook his head. "No, sir. More than likely some isolated farm or ranch has been raided by the Chogolas."

"Then let's hurry forward to do our duty," Blackburn said. He waved to Pullini. "Sound the *Charge!*"

Pullini, who spoke Italian when he became especially excited, acknowledged the order with a curt, *"Si, Signore Capitano!"*

"Hold it!" Guy shouted.

"What the hell do you mean?" Blackburn demanded.

"It will be too late, sir," Guy replied in a tone of resignation. "This is the part of Indian warfare that I hate the most."

"Explain yourself, Sergeant."

"There will be nothing to do but bury the dead, Captain," Guy explained. "Or at least what is left of them."

Blackburn started to get Pullini's attention again, then he quickly changed his mind. "Very well. Let's investigate."

The column moved forward once more. It took an hour to reach the smoke, which by then had dissipated into weak, restless wisps whipped around by the breeze. Guy had been correct. A farm house, burned to charred sticks, sat in a circle of scorched grass. Two white blobs, looking like red painted porcupines, lay punctured with countless arrows.

When the company reached the vicinity several men, including Capt. Gordon Blackburn, quickly slid out of their saddles to vomit. Two males had been mutilated beyond imagination. Nothing but bloody meat remained where the victims once had faces. Their genitals, chopped away, had been laid in the cavities of their disemboweled stomachs.

"Corporal Hansen!" Guy called out. "Take two men and look around. See if there are more bodies or possibly survivors."

Hansen spat. "There won't be no damn survivors, Sergeant. You know that."

"See what you can find," Guy said.

Blackburn, his eyes watery, rinsed out his mouth with a drink from his canteen. "Do those devils always do that?"

"Yes, sir, when they get a chance," Guy said. "They believe enemies that are mutilated go to the afterlife to spend eternity in such a state."

Blackburn, to his credit, forced himself to take another look. "One is—was—a man," he said. "But the other couldn't be more than a boy of ten or twelve."

Hansen returned from his task. "They ain't nobody else, but I seen some stuff that a woman or girl might have owned. I seen some dresses and a mirror." He shook his head. "Them Chogolas prob'ly took her away wit'em. Poor woman!"

Blackburn's face hardened. "God! I've love to catch up with those heathens."

"Don't worry, sir," Guy said. "Before tomorrow's sunset you'll be a fully-qualified Indian fighter."

The conversation was interrupted by the arrival of the rest of the squadron. Over a hundred and twenty troops moved into the small farm yard, making their number appear even larger.

The commanding officer dispersed his men around the area in the unlikely event that the Indians might return. Company C, now back in the larger group, moved to its usual position within the large column.

A squadron trumpeter sought out Captain Blackburn. "Major Scott's compliments, sir, and would you please report to him immediately."

"Well," Blackburn said. "It looks like this war is really starting to roll along now." He nodded to Guy. "Sergeant DuBose, take over the company until my return."

"Yes, sir," Guy replied. He went immediately to personally inspect each man on the defensive line. This was done not out of necessity or a devotion to duty. Staying busy at anything helped keep the constant thoughts of Pauline at bay.

CHAPTER 13

The First Squadron commander, a dour teetotaler named Maj. Standish Scott, had begun to weary of the pursuit. As an old veteran, he recognized the fact that the Indians were leading him and his men on a chase of their own design. He was also aware that keeping his command together kept the pace down. He decided to split off two of the four companies in an attempt to circle the Chogolas and force them into a direct southerly direction where he and the main body of the squadron could catch up with them more easily.

One of the companies chosen to be a flying column was Company C under the command of Capt. Gordon Blackburn and his two sergeants DuBose and Tate. They accepted the orders with feelings of anticipation. It appeared to these senior men, and their subordinates too, that there was every chance for a battle. Their assignment was to angle off to the west until contact was made. The men grimly checked their weapons and ammunition in preparation for the fighting that seemed inevitable.

But the excitement slackened thirty-six hours later as it became apparent that the situation would probably remain unchanged. The troops slouched in their saddles and even the flankers and advance guard daydreamed during the slow advance across the mind-dulling prairie. Then, in a few seconds, the boredom was suddenly dashed.

The first indication of trouble was the appearance of a lone Indian warrior on the skyline.

On this fourth day in the saddle, the C Company cavalrymen suddenly became alert and exhilarated with a mixture of excitement and fear. Although only a single enemy, the lone warrior was a herald of a lot more to come. The Indian rode toward them emitting wild yells. Suddenly he stopped and turned his horse around. The Chogola pulled up his breech cloth to bare his buttocks. He patted them contemptuously at the soldiers.

"The son of a bitch," Guy said. He stood in his stirrups. "Flankers in!" he hollered. Then he gestured to Pullini. "Sound *Recall,* damn it! And keep it up until all the flankers and the advance guard have returned to the column."

"Certamente, mi sergente!" Pullini put the instrument to his lips and began an interrupted series of the bugle call while turning his horse around in a circle to make sure the outriders could hear him.

"What the hell's going on, Sergeant?" Blackburn demanded. He pointed outward. "Who is that lone idiot out there baring his arse at us?"

Guy ignored him. "Columns of sections!" he commanded. "To the left, march!"

Sgt. Harry Tate led his section up into position along

the left side of Guy's. The men in both units had pulled their carbines from the saddleboots. All faced outward, ready for whatever might happen.

Blackburn was working himself into a rage. "Sergeant DuBose! I demand—"

"Here come the flankers!" somebody yelled out.

The half-dozen men who had been screening the column now galloped in madly in answer to Pullini's persistent bugling. Guy, speaking to himself more than anyone else, muttered, "Come on, you fellows! Come on! Come on!"

Scattered shots sounded from the distance. One of the troopers reeled in his saddle, then he seemed to regain his balance. But after a few more yards he fell from his horse and hit the ground hard, kicking up dust and debris.

Corporal Hansen abruptly spurred his horse and broke out of the column. He urged his mount into a gallop straight for the fallen man. The men cheered his effort as several Indians now made bold appearances.

Guy became infuriated. "Donovan! Horn! Come with me!" He streaked out after Hansen with the two troopers following. They could see the corporal rein up by the fallen man and leap off his horse.

The Indians had also sighted the Dane. They turned their full fury on him in the guise of barking rifles. Hansen leaped back into his saddle and headed back for the company. Guy and his two companions wheeled their own horses around in time to join him for the dash back to safety.

"The fellow is dead!" Hansen shouted to Guy. The four men rejoined their comrades in a pounding cloud of dust.

Guy was so angry that he reached out and grabbed the chevrons on Hansen's left arm. He ripped them away in a fury. "God damn your soul, Hansen! You'll not be an N.C.O. in my section, and if you ever do that again I'll have you court-martialed and sent to prison!"

"But, Sergeant," Hansen protested. "I wanted to help that man. He was down."

"And dead," Guy said. "You risked the battle formation by leaving your post. If we had been hit from the other side, your squad would have been leaderless."

Blackburn, who had been turning back and forth aimlessly between the two sections, finally settled down and joined Guy and Harry Tate in the middle of the double column. He had pulled his pistol from his holster in readiness for fighting. "Do you think the rest of the squadron will be here shortly, Sergeant?" the captain asked.

"Yes, sir," Guy answered. "If they hear the shooting." Guy could tell from the captain's conduct that he had no intention of exercising command.

A hundred warriors had appeared on the scene. They'd strung themselves out and were galloping in a wide, but ever decreasing circle around the soldiers. Guy could recognize several of the Chogolas that he knew personally—Lame Elk, Two Ponies, Old Bow, and Young Buffalo. The latter was the one who had been whipped by Blackburn's orders. Guy knew the Comanche would love to get his hands on Blackburn.

Guy ordered the men to dismount and make their horses lie down. This had been done in drill many times, but the rising crescendo of shooting made several of the animals balk. The defensive position was not as precise as done in training, but now the men could fire from the prone position using their mounts' bodies for cover.

Several of the Indians became bolder and rode directly toward the troopers, brandishing their weapons. Blackburn, who still held his pistol ready, had calmed down but was making no effort to take over from Guy. In fact, when a lone warrior galloped so close that it was easy to make out his facial features, the captain consulted his senior sergeant. "What is that rascal doing, DuBose?"

"You see that hooped device in his right hand?" Guy asked. "That's a coup stick. He can earn prestige and battle honors by tapping his enemies with it during battle."

The Indian, now being encouraged by his shouting friends farther back, came closer. Then, as if suddenly inspired, he kicked his horse's flanks and made a dash toward the troops.

Several carbines cracked, but the warrior continued on his way straight toward the soldiers' position. He concentrated hard on this dangerous task, not even emitting a war whoop, as he headed deeper into danger. Suddenly he wheeled to his left and leaned down smacking one of the soldiers so hard that the man's hat flew off.

Yelling triumphantly the Indian raced back toward his tribesmen. They shrieked their approval and admiration for the brave war deed. This reception encouraged another of the warriors to try. The Chogola rode in a straight line toward the soldiers, his coup stick held in his outstretched hand.

Blackburn was confused. "Those savages seem to be losing track of the tactical situation."

"Yes, sir," Guy agreed. "That is one of their disadvantages. Besides a lack of discipline, they let individual honors outweigh the need for immediate victory."

The Indian continued on his way, drawing closer and closer. Now even the soldiers appreciated his bravery. He brandished no weapons of destruction, only seeking esteem rather than blood. He finally drew up to within twenty-five yards.

Blackburn raised his pistol and carefully aimed. He fired, and the ball hit true. It knocked the Indian over the rump of his horse to collapse to the dusty prairie grass. The captain smiled. "Target shooting has always been a hobby of mine."

The spell was broken for the Chogolas. They went back to fighting the battle on the white man's terms. The soldiers began sporadic shooting, but Guy didn't want that. "Cease fire! Cease fire!" he shouted. Even Tate's section obeyed. "One round, lock and load!"

Those who didn't have a live bullet in the chambers of the single-shot Springfields quickly inserted one.

"Listen up!" Guy warned them. "Stand steady!"

The Indians were once again circling, firing from horseback and not doing much damage. The poorly aimed shots either zinged through the air or plowed into the dirt yards short of the soldiers. After five minutes of this useless activity, a half dozen of the warriors banded together. They left their circle and charged. And they came with rifles, not coup sticks.

Since they were coming straight toward Harry Tate's men, the sergeant took command. "Don't anticipate my orders, God damn your eyes!" he yelled. "Wait for it! Take aim! Now make sure them sight pitchers is good! Wait for it! Wait for it! Ready! Fire!"

Twenty carbines belched smoke and steel. The volley zipped across the short distance like a swarm of angry hornets. The slugs slapped into the assaulting Indians, dumping four of them to the ground. The two survivors wisely turned their horses and fled back to their circling friends.

"What the hell did they do that for?" Captain asked no one in particular. "It would have been to their advantage for the entire group to hit one side of our position."

Tate, grinning, looked back at him. "They don't work good together, sir. And that's why this land is gonna belong to white folks before long."

But, almost as if to make a liar of the sergeant, a large group broke off and launched a thundering, shrieking attack. It was Guy's turn that time. These Comanche braves did not fire until they were much closer.

Although the shooting was not highly accurate, it was at the right height to hit men lying prone. Three soldiers were struck. One died instantly, his skull exploding with such violence that his hat seemed to leap into the air of its own accord. Another, hit in the shoulder, instinctively jumped up and was hit again. The final wound killed him. The third man caught a bullet in the hand. He cursed and slid deeper behind his horse.

Guy waited until he thought the time was right. "Take aim!" He said nothing else until the roaring charge had reached a point less than fifty yards' distance from the defenders. "Fire!"

Once again coordinated hell blasted outward from the troops and cut down Indians like stalks of wheat.

The luckier Chogolas, a bit more than half of whom had made the attempt, withdrew out of range. The rest of the warriors joined them. The sudden cessation of shooting and shouting made the atmosphere seem eerily silent.

Blackburn, his battle lust lit, walked forward to stand in the front ranks of the soldiers. One of the men looked up at him. "That was nice shooting, sir."

"Yes, sir, Cap'n," another joined in. "You shot 'at damn Injun off his hoss with one pull o' the trigger."

Blackburn felt a swell of manly pride. "That's the way to handle those buggers, men," he replied. "What's that old saying? 'The only good Indian is a dead Indian', right?"

"Yes, sir!" they hollered.

Guy joined him. "I think that's the end of it, sir. But we'd better keep the men ready just in case."

"End of it, hell! What's the matter with those sons of bitches, Sergeant?" Blackburn asked. "Have we frightened them?"

"No, sir," Guy answered. "The Indian picks his time and place for battle. If they feel any fear, it's because of what they might consider bad medicine about this place. They haven't been too lucky here."

"I'll say they haven't," Blackburn remarked with a laugh.

Guy had the men wait for an hour. A few minutes after he ordered them to remount, the remainder of the squadron appeared. The sight of the dead Indians and the two dead soldiers caused a flurry of excitement among the arrivals. The commanding officer with his adjutant rode into Company C's small position.

Major Scott took Blackburn's salute. "How did it

152

go, Captain?"

"Fine, sir," Blackburn said. His political savvy came to the fore. "I was heavily outnumbered and surrounded, but stood fast. Although I had two men killed and one wounded, you can easily tell I gave more than I took."

"Very well, Captain," the major said. "I would appreciate a written report upon our return to Fort Alexander."

Blackburn was disappointed. "Are we not going to continue the pursuit, sir?"

"I'm afraid not. We have gone past our patrol boundaries now. Fort Richardson will have to deal with Lame Elk this far south. We shall retrace our steps back to hearth, home, and headquarters."

The squadron held a brief burial service for the two dead men. The Service for the Dead was read from the bible, and Captain Blackburn praised the men for their bravery. One was an Irish rowdy from Boston and the other a young, rather sensitive Swiss fellow. The uniforms in which they died had made them brothers.

After the quick funeral, Blackburn asked Guy to take a short walk with him. Guy vaguely wondered if it concerned Pauline. Perhaps she had told the captain they had once been fiancees. But Blackburn was all army business.

"Sergeant, perhaps we didn't get off on the right foot together," he said. "But relationships between officer and soldier are really formed in the fire and steel of battle, are they not?"

"Yes, sir," Guy answered. But, as a veteran, he had recognized that the fight with the Chogolas was the captain's first introduction to war.

153

"We have started over, Sergeant DuBose," Blackburn said. "If you are loyal and obedient, there is no reason why your own military fortunes cannot rise with my own." He smiled in a magnanimous way. "Now! That's open and above board, is it not?"

"Yes, sir," Guy replied, the expression on his face noncommittal. "But I prefer a professional, caste-conscious relationship. In this case, I do not feel even a proper form of comradeship would work out between us."

Blackburn was angered by the rebuff. "Very well! You've just made a terrible misjudgment, Sergeant DuBose. But perhaps you are correct. At any rate I prefer that you remain an underling and a servant to do my bidding. Understood?"

"Perfectly, sir."

"Fine. Now let's get back to the company and prepare them for the ride back to garrison," Blackburn said. "We've still a few days of riding before we'll see that main gate again. I am sure that my wife or I will have a chore or two for you at Fort Alexander in the coming days."

Suddenly the one thought he'd been especially fighting to subdue leaped into his mind with full realization: Blackburn was returning to Pauline. Guy clenched his teeth and saluted, then hurried back to the men.

CHAPTER 14

"My! You're quite a handy young lady, Laura Lee!" Pauline exclaimed. "Those curtains are lovely. Where on earth did you find them?"

"They was left over from Cap'n Wayne," Laura Lee explained as she finished arranging the window coverings. "My mama washed 'em for him, but he said he din't need 'em no more." She smiled shyly and added, "I made 'em myself."

"They are lovely," Pauline said.

"I'm right pleased you like 'em, Mrs. Blackburn," Laura Lee said stepping down from the chair she'd been standing on to tend the chore.

"You're certainly going to be a wonderful wife to some lucky young man," Pauline said.

Laura Lee Tate was fifteen years old. Though still a bit tomboyish and gangly, she showed every indication of growing into an attractive woman. Her braided hair was straw-colored, and light freckles danced across her nose. "Mrs. Blackburn," she said. "I was wondering that if'n you ever got the chance, could you teach me to use that sewing doo-dad o' your'n?"

"My sewing machine?" Pauline asked. She referred to her Singer Continuous Stitch Sewing Machine. It was one of her favorite possessions. When she and her husband put their belongings into storage, Pauline insisted that the small contraption go with her. She was pleased that Laura Lee liked it too. "Of course, honey. I'd be pleased. Perhaps we might do a few things together since you love to sew so much. I adore making dresses myself. Wouldn't it be fun if we made one special for you?"

"Oh, yes, Mrs. Blackburn! Maybe I could git one made up for the soljers' ball," Laura Lee said. "I think somebody might ask me to go with him."

"Oh, Laura Lee! Do you have a beau?"

"Sorta," she answered. "He's a soljer over to A Comp'ny. The only problem is that he's skeered to death o' my pa. But he said he was gonna come over to the house and ask me to the dance anyhow."

"I'm not surprised," Pauline said. "Now don't you worry. We'll fashion something very stylish and beautiful for you. Your soldier boy is going to find you the prettiest girl at the ball."

"You reckon I could really look—well, perty like?" she asked. Laura Lee thought Pauline was the most beautiful woman she had ever seen.

"Of course," Pauline said. "There is nothing we cannot do with my sewing machine."

"Me and mama sew clothes but we got to use our ol' needle and thread," Laura Lee said. "It takes perty near forever."

"Well, we'll quickly turn out a very nice dress for you," Pauline said. "Maybe even more. I think it would

156

be a wonderful idea if you had a party dress, then a very nice one to go to church in."

"Oh, Mrs. Blackburn!" Laura Lee smiled in absolute delight, then her expression faded somewhat. She hesitated before she spoke again. "Mrs. Blackburn, you been real nice to me."

"Why we're friends, child," Pauline said.

"I'm glad o' that 'cause I got a favor to ask o' you."

"What in the world is it?" Pauline inquired.

"I'd like to leave directly after fixing supper in the evenings, if you please."

"Why is that?"

"Excuse me, Missus Blackburn, but your man makes me real nervous," Laura Lee said.

Pauline understood. She walked over and embraced the girl knowing how she must feel. "Now don't you worry any about the captain. He's gruff, but he won't say anything mean or do anything mean to you."

"I'm sorry, Mrs. Blackburn."

"I understand, child. Don't you worry, hear?" She laughed lightly. "He's sort of like an old dog who growls to himself. It may sound gruff but he won't bite."

"Yes, ma'am," Laura Lee said. "I got to go now. Mama wants some help with the washing. She says she thinks it best to have it all finished when the soljers come back from patrol."

"All right, dear," Pauline said. "Don't you do any fretting over my husband. You won't have a thing to do with him, understand?"

"Yes, ma'am. I feel better now getting it out in the open," the girl said. "I knowed you'd do something 'bout it one way or the other."

"Good. Run along. I'll see you in the morning." Pauline let the girl out the door, then walked back to the kitchen area of the three-room home that she and her husband rated. She knew she would have to ask Gordon to be more civil toward Laura Lee. He had a natural tendency to be surly, and the youngster didn't really understand that he was only barely aware of her presence.

Pauline walked back to the last room of the three. This was the kitchen. A pot of coffee, set on the stove kept hot by coals, waited for her. She poured a cup, then sat down at the table. Her mind returned to Guy DuBose, as it always had even before her trip out to Fort Alexander.

The shock of seeing him standing there in the train depot had been bad enough at the time. Later on the full realization settled in, giving Pauline long bouts of sadness and regret. During the patrol with her husband gone, she'd had some private moments to let her emotions go their own way. She wept bitterly in a combination of grief, happiness, and relief that Guy had really survived the war.

Pauline had her memories—good and bad—that really started after the typhoid epidemic that carried away her parents. Orphaned at the age of seventeen, she had been forced to move in with another branch of the family. She found a great degree of contentment there, however. Her cousins Selby and Glenna Berger had welcomed her with sincere warmth and affection.

But her true happiness blossomed when handsome Guy DuBose came into her life. Her most delightful memory was of the warm evening when he awkwardly approached her with his declaration of undying love

158

and affection. He'd been so sweet and comically pathetic at the same time that Pauline had wanted to laugh with joy and clutch him close to her and whisper of her own love for him. But, being a proper belle, she had observed propriety's rules and accepted his inexpert but gallant courtship as a lady should.

The gaiety of her life during those short, giddy months still caused her heart to flutter when she remembered them: Waltzing with her love across broad ballrooms at the military dances of the Zouave regiment; walking arm-in-arm with him along the banks of the Cooper River; or sitting by his side during dinner parties at the Berger plantation.

She had been so proud to be his sweetheart, and she knew that many a girl's heartfelt hopes had been dashed when her uncle announced the engagement at that most wonderful party just before Christmas in 1860.

But all of that came to a crashing end with the attack on Fort Sumter.

She remembered Charleston had been hard hit early by the Yankee naval blockade after the war started and the militia marched off to serve the Confederate States of America. The little amount of goods that got in or out was transported by smugglers who did the work more out of a love of profit than for patriotism. Prices of common goods shot up when those articles were suddenly no longer common. Luxuries at first became priced out of all proportion, then they became nonexistent. Her personal life was especially hard hit.

Besides having the man she loved with all her heart taken away from her by the circumstances of the conflict, her own status—which was worse than modest to begin with—deteriorated even more.

The Bergers' own fortunes fell. High taxes and demands for goods to send to the army put a horrible strain on her uncle's plantation. Where once there had been what seemed like unceasing plenty, there were suddenly shortages and want. Clothing was impossible to obtain while necessities like food became dearer and dearer. The white inhabitants of the Berger household found their former extravagant lives reduced to meager existences. Hunger struck everyone when food stocks ran low. Butchered livestock could not be replaced and the seed to grow food also all but disappeared. There was no use in trying to raise tobacco or cotton. With Federal ships arrogantly sailing up and down the coast of South Carolina, there was no way to get those products to European markets.

Pauline began to feel she was a strain on her aunt and uncle early on. She was one more mouth to be fed. Untrained to be anything but a lady, the only commercial skill she'd learned was sewing. But there was no cloth with which to make clothing. The young woman thought things had gotten as bad as they could until that horrible day that Selby Berger came home on a prisoner exchange treaty.

He had been horribly maimed in battle. Emaciated and wasted away, he was brought home to the plantation on a pallet. One leg had been amputated and his other wounds, barely healed, had turned the rest of his body to scarred pulp. His voice was so weak it was no more than a whisper, but the words he spoke to Pauline had the impact of a demonic scream:

"Oh, Pauline, honey," he'd struggled to say. "I'm so sorry but we've lost our Guy."

The world came to a complete stop for one horrible second. Her mind tried to deny what she heard, but Selby continued to speak.

"It was the last day at Gettysburg," he wheezed. "We'd formed up with Pickett's division for a last try at the Yankee lines. They threw everything they had at us and we took it all. The charge had come to a stop and I glanced down the line of the regiment to see how things stood. That was when I saw Guy crumple and fall. There was so many of the boys down. We couldn't even bury them properly. We had to leave their bodies in Yankee hands."

Pauline had stood up and walked up the stairs to her room in the back of the house. That was the end of it all as far as she was concerned. The war, losing her parents, all the suffering could have been borne had Guy survived. The love she had for him was the one source of strength that sustained her. Now that was gone.

Selby's own death a month later coincided with the arrival of victorious Union troops. They moved into the area in a manner which the Romans must have done in Britain. The Berger home was taken over for a headquarters. Before long the family was forced to stay in the former slave quarters while blue-coated officers boldly moved into the old plantation house.

Among the officers was a dark somber lieutenant named Gordon Blackburn. At first he was aloof as he went about his duties. But as time went by, when their paths crossed, he began to issue curt but polite greetings to her. She knew that this officer found her attractive and desirable. It was much the same way that she had fathomed Guy's affections for her several years earlier.

Soon Blackburn's attentions grew bolder and he found reasons to draw her into conversations regarding the plantation grounds such as locations of specific buildings, the best routes to various points in the vicinity, and other business-like inquiries.

The next progression in their relationship was useless gifts such as flowers. This was followed by his request to her uncle to come calling on the young woman. The elder Berger, still a staunch secessionist, refused in anger. Then Blackburn changed his tactics. Instead of flowers, he began sending food. The one thing the Yankees had plenty of was the material necessities of life. It was at that point that Pauline's mind seemed to drift away from her.

She wanted to get away from the plantation and the memories of her beloved Guy. She was a strain on the Berger family, and she could not tolerate it anymore. Pauline wanted more than anything to get out of those horrible, demeaning circumstances. The most desirable thing she could imagine would be to flee those surroundings forever, to start again and somehow put it all behind her. Her broken heart and aching soul would mend. But in a world where a woman was not even allowed to vote, there was little she could do to sustain herself at any more than a bare existence.

Blackburn continued pressing his courtship on her, and his intentions were honorable. By then she realized that her chance for a dignified escape would be in marriage to the Yankee officer. Ignoring her family's rage, Pauline encouraged the man even though she fully realized that she would never love him. It made no difference, she reasoned, for she would never love any other man after Guy DuBose.

When Blackburn proposed, she accepted even though she knew the marriage would separate her forever from the same people who had been so kind and loving toward her. After the day Pauline married Gordon Blackburn in the small ceremony conducted by an army chaplain, she would never hear from the Bergers or any of her former South Carolinian friends again for the rest of her life.

Her joining with this dark stranger from the north cut her completely and permanently out of their lives. She was worse than a traitor in their eyes for she had betrayed and sullied a fine young man's memory. Pauline knew she could never make them understand what drove her to such a desperate decision, or convince them that it was best for them too.

Pauline did not have to bear being near her family for long. Blackburn, a regular army officer, was transferred to the adjutant general's department in Washington City. This was done through the influence of Blackburn's father who was active in New York state politics. She met his family, wealthy New Englanders, and they coolly accepted the beautiful southern woman into their family. Through the period after the end of the fighting, the Blackburns never warmed to her. In spite of this subtle snubbing, her life was pleasant compared to the war years. Pauline wanted for nothing—save true love—and she moved into the political and military social whirl of the nation's capital. Her upbringing had made her a natural flirt, and she did this outrageously with Blackburn's superiors. These old colonels and generals enjoyed the brief attentions of so lovely a young lady, and the couple was in constant demand for dinner parties and dances.

Blackburn was quickly promoted to the rank of captain and finally received brevets through major and lieutenant colonel. His responsibilities increased until he was assigned the prestigious position of maintaining and recommending the army's strength and duty assignment lists. He even had two men to work as his assistants. His future and permanent stay in Washington City seemed bright and permanent.

Then the bottom fell out.

Two major generals with opposing views on the conduct of pacifying the Indians in the still untamed west had been sparring with each other for years. Their conflict finally came to an open clash. Blackburn, eager to hitch his wagon to the victor's star, chose the officer whose policy included the ousting of Gen. Phil Sheridan. Sheridan, knowing of the plot, called in favors and fired a few powerful political guns of his own. This barrage fell heavily on his foe causing the man's early retirement from active duty. Naturally, this included the disgraced general's supporters as well.

Brevet Lt. Col. Gordon Blackburn was one of those to feel the sting of Sheridan's fury. Within one week he was removed from his plush posting and assigned to an obscure office that dealt with the post non-commissioned staff of unmanned military facilities. Chastised and humiliated, the once popular officer noticed a sharp decline in social invitations and several downright snubs not only from ranking officers but subordinates too. Then the orders assigning him to a distant cavalry regiment out on the Texas frontier arrived. It was tantamount to the end of his career.

The west was full of dead-ends for officers. Only those with plenty of luck in the ceaseless, dirty wars against the hostile tribes could hope to garner enough glory and publicity to gain promotion. It appeared that Blackburn's bright star had at last burned out.

Now, confused and heartbroken, Pauline Berger Blackburn sat in the kitchen of the home she shared with a husband she did not love. She sadly sipped her coffee, her heart full of regret at the impetuous decision that had ruined the chance for a truly happy life. A sudden flurry of activity outside caught her attention. Pauline got up and walked to the window.

The troops had returned to Fort Alexander.

CHAPTER 15

The supply wagons, heavily escorted by a full company of cavalry, rolled through Fort Alexander's main gate. Lieutenant Robertson, the regimental quartermaster, had submitted emergency supply and munition requisitions after Lame Elk's breakout from the Red River Agency. These requests had been hastily answered by the Texas Military Department who shipped the items to Dahlquart. The vehicles had been dispatched under heavy guard for the needed and valuable goods.

The sentries on duty were startled when a man, obviously a civilian, hollered down to them from one of the wagons. "Say, soldiers, where might I find Col. Gordon Blackburn?" He clambered down to the ground from the high seat.

"There ain't no colonel by that name here," the trooper responded as he dully watched the driver toss down a couple of large suitcases to the man. "The onliest colonel we got is a feller named Gatley."

The civilian was thoughtful for a moment. "I

presume there is an officer named Blackburn, is there not?"

"Oh, yeah. We got one and he's a dandy shot," the other sentry answered.

"That's the gentleman I'm looking for," the man said. "He's a crack marksman with a pistol."

"Well, if his name's Blackburn, he ain't a colonel. He's a captain."

"I see. Then where might I find Captain Blackburn?"

"Well, now, on a Sunday afternoon after Church Call, he'll be off duty," the sentry said. "I'd reckon he'd be at his quarters."

"Fine," the civilian said. "Would you be kind enough to point out the location?"

"Over there is Officers Row," the soldier said.

The man looked in the direction indicated. It appeared to be a quarter of a mile away. "Say, I'll give two-bits to anybody that will carry these bags of mine over there."

"Hell, Mister! I'm your man," one of the soldiers said.

But his friend cautioned him. "You ain't supposed to leave your post without being properly relieved, Eugene."

"I don't give a shit. Two bits will get me five beers over to the sutler's store. I'll be back afore the corp'ral of the guard gets wise," the soldier said. He leaned his carbine against the sentry shack. "Let's go, Mister."

The two moved rapidly as the wayward guard set a panicky pace. They covered the ground quickly. When they arrived, the soldier held out his hand for his money. "Don't knock on that door 'til I'm gone. I don't want Cap'n Blackburn to know what I done."

"I pledge my silence, young man," the civilian said. He flipped a coin to the trooper. He waited until the kid had gone a distance before he rapped on the door.

It was answered by Blackburn. The captain's dark countenance lit up. "Morris! Thank God you're here."

"Hello, Gordon," Morris Kramer said. "Help me get my luggage inside, will you, old man? I would tell you how I got it here, but I am in another's strict confidence."

Blackburn smiled. "Some soldier strayed from his proper duty no doubt."

"Indeed," Kramer said taking one bag while Blackburn took the other. He stepped inside, then broke into an even wider smile. "Pauline! How wonderful to see you."

Pauline, dressed in a riding habit, did not suppress her pleasure. "Morris Kramer, I've been waiting on pins and needles since Gordon told me he had written you. But I never thought you would leave Washington City."

"Don't forget, my dear, that I will go anywhere my professional interest takes me," Kramer said.

Pauline eyed him carefully. "And what 'professional interest' is there for a journalist of the *Washington Daily Chronicle* away out here in Texas?"

"An Indian war, my dear," Kramer said. "I took Gordon's letter to my editor and it was decided that I would do a series of articles regarding the campaigning done by the army out here."

"I fear we haven't much in the way of lodging to offer you," Pauline said. "We have only three rooms. A living room, a bedroom, and a kitchen all set in a neat row."

169

"She's right, old man," Blackburn added. "The very best I could do was a bed in our parlor. You'll have to endure an outdoor privy as well."

Kramer laughed. "Just like my old farm home in Pennsylvania." He gave the woman a quizzical look. "Are you going riding, Pauline? You're certainly dressed for it."

"Yes," she answered smiling. "For the first time since our arrival at Fort Alexander. It hasn't been considered safe until the hostiles left the area. I am going out with two more of the officers' wives."

"I've arranged for an escort," Blackburn explained. "One of my sergeants, an ex-Confederate by the name of DuBose, will be their protector."

Pauline's face blanched white. "DuBose? You didn't tell me *he* was going with us!"

Blackburn frowned. "What in the world does it matter to you?" He considered her words. "Do you know him, Pauline?"

She shook her head. "No—no, of course not. I'm sorry, Gordon. I—well, I just thought we ladies would be by ourselves."

"My dear, it is not that safe," Blackburn said. "I'm almost sorry I came up with the idea. The impudent fellow DuBose most certainly did not like the assignment. In fact, he was nearly insubordinate in his protests of the task. I brought the full weight of my office and rank to bear. In a situation like that, one can't let a soldier get the idea that he's won over you."

The sound of approaching feminine conversation caught the three people's attention. Blackburn answered the light rapping on the door. "Mrs. Robertson and Mrs. Harris, please come in," he said in an untypical display of cordiality. "May I present my friend Mr. Morris Kramer of Washington City."

"How do you do, ladies," Kramer said.

Minnie Robertson and Violet Harris were fascinated by so many people only recently arrived from the East. They began what promised to become a prolonged conversation, but Pauline quickly interrupted. "I am really anxious to go riding. It's been such a long, long time." She started for the door, holding it open in an undeniable hint to leave.

"Yes, we should go," Minnie Robertson said. "It was very nice meeting you, Mister Kramer."

"We must have you to our home for dinner," Violet Harris said.

Pauline quickly ushered them outside. The three strode side-by-side down Officers Row and past the regimental headquarters. Violet smiled impishly. "Guess who is to be our escort?"

Minnie looked at her. "Don't tell me!"

"Yes! Sergeant DuBose," Violet said. She looked across her friend at Pauline. "He is a most handsome fellow, Pauline. But you should know that. He is in your husband's company, is he not?"

"Yes," Pauline answered. "In fact, he was in charge of the escort that fetched me from Dahlquart."

Minnie giggled. "For heaven's sakes! I feel wicked!"

"Yes! Imagine married ladies carrying on like this," Violet said. "And about an enlisted man too."

Pauline almost blurted out that Guy had been a captain in the Confederate army, but she stopped herself. When they arrived at the stables they found Sgt. Guy DuBose waiting with four horses saddled.

Three, with sidesaddles, were hitched to a rail outside the building. "Good afternoon," Guy greeted them in a somber voice. "Your mounts are ready." One by one he helped them settle in for the ride. Pauline was the last. She purposely gripped his arm with extra effort as he smoothly helped her up into position.

"Thank you very much," Pauline said.

Guy swung up onto his own horse. "Is there any particular place you would care to go?"

Minnie shook her head. "This dreary country is all the same. Why don't we just make a wide—a very wide—circuit of the post?"

"Wait," Violet said. "Let's go out to the knoll. We can see best there. That way Pauline can get the finest view possible of her new home."

"Very well," Minnie conceded. "But let's go the long way."

"Yes, ma'am," Guy said. "Please lead on."

They left the stable area and turned south to skirt the parade ground. After going past the post chapel and entering the open prairie, they broke into a canter. All three of the ladies were expert riders. They swayed gracefully with the horses' movements as the animals loped easily over the gently rolling terrain. Gradually they veered to the west until they were out of sight of Fort Alexander. Only then did Minnie Robertson, in the lead, turn north.

The excursion continued for an hour until a slight turn to the east brought the group to an easily recognized and noteworthy rise in the flat plains country. When they reached the apex, all brought their horses to a halt.

"Look, Pauline," Minnie said. "This is the best view

available of our dear, dear Fort Alexander."

Pauline could see the entire post and a good portion of the countryside all the way to a hazy glimpse of the Red River. "It's so plain," she said. "Yet at the same time there is a sort of beauty to it."

Guy, remaining silent, could see the creek and the rosebud tree where he liked to sit for solitary drunks. Now the very cause of those bouts of sad intoxication was sitting on a horse beside him.

Minnie had also seen the creek. She was an adventurous lady. "Let's race down to that tree and back!"

"Yes!" Violet said.

"Oh, dear," Pauline said. "Not me. I am more used to orderly riding trails I'm afraid. But I shall be most happy to act as referee."

"Done!" Minnie said. She looked at Guy. "Sergeant DuBose, will you start us off?"

"Get ready," Guy said solemnly. "Get set. Go."

The two ladies smacked their horses with their quirts and set off. Pauline watched them for a few short seconds, then she turned a beseeching face toward Guy. "Forgive me, Guy. I thought you were dead!"

Guy, intently watching the racers, said nothing.

Pauline pulled on the reins walking her horse closer to his. "Guy, we haven't much time. I still love you. I never stopped. Even after I thought you had been killed."

His face was stone. "Why did you marry him?"

"I can't explain it now. Not here," Pauline said. "Tell me you don't hate me, Guy. Please."

His heart melted and he swallowed hard. "No. No. I don't hate you. I thought I did. Oh, God, why did all

173

this happen?"

"Guy?" There was no denying the pleading in her voice. "Guy?" It was an entreaty for him to speak what was in his heart. "I must know."

He knew what she wanted him to say and he wanted to say it too. "I love you, Pauline."

Minnie and Violet had reached the creek and turned.

"What are we going to do?" she asked.

"Let me think," he said. His emotions had been jerked around by this sudden realization that Pauline still loved him. A terribly complicated situation was in the making, and it required cool, clear thought. That was something he was incapable of at that moment. He was torn between happiness and sadness knowing she was wed to another man. "I must sort it all out."

"I love you, Guy."

"I love you, Pauline," he said. "We must stay in touch somehow. I'll work it out."

"Yes, darling, yes!"

The other two now rapidly approached, drawing near as the pounding of their horses' hooves sent clods of dark dirt flying behind them. They streaked past, then quickly wheeled and came to a walk. Minnie called out, "Who won?"

Pauline looked at Guy. She whispered, "I didn't notice."

"Violet," he whispered back.

"Violet won," Pauline called.

"Hooray for me," Violet Harris shouted.

"Oh, poo!" Minnie complained. "If there weren't a man present, I'd say a lot more, believe me."

Guy laughed. "I appreciate your kind consideration, ma'am."

174

"Well!" Violet said. "Your mood has improved. I thought you were going to be a grumpy old bear all afternoon."

"Not at all," Guy said. "Shall we continue the outing?"

They resumed their trek to the east, without making any more stops. Guy and Pauline gave each other furtive, longing looks. They were careful in the company of two very experienced, gossiping army wives like Minnie Robertson and Violet Harris.

After a complete circuit which took them past Soap Suds Row and once more back to the post chapel, they returned to the stables.

Guy helped the ladies dismount. This time, in clandestine pleasure, he and Pauline gave each other's hands an extra squeeze before releasing. A young private appeared and took all four horses, leading them over to the corral for a cooling down.

"Thank you for your gallant company, Sergeant," Minnie Robertson said.

"My pleasure, ladies," Guy said. "Good afternoon."

The three wives walked back to Officers Row. Because Pauline's husband was a captain and outranked Lieutenants Robertson and Harris, the Blackburn quarters were closer to regimental headquarters. Pauline, almost giddy with joy, made her goodbys and almost skipped to the door.

But her mood sobered at the sight of her husband and Morris Kramer. They sat in the parlor, evidently having been in deep conversation. Her greeting was simple. "Hello."

Blackburn looked at her in a detached manner. "Hello, Pauline. Morris and I have been having quite a serious conversation."

"One of benefit for all of us however," Kramer added.

"Yes. I'm going to see that he is given the best opportunities to get a full exposure in this campaign against Lame Elk," Blackburn said.

"I see," Pauline said. "And what benefits shall you reap, Gordon?"

Kramer answered. "I am going to write him up in the most glowing terms possible. When these dispatches hit Washington City and are published in the *Daily Chronicle,* the readership will be totally convinced that he is the finest Indian fighter ever produced by West Point."

"That readership," Blackburn added, "consists of many politicians and other bigwigs." He smiled. "That means our return to the War Department is only a matter of a few months, my dear."

"Exactly," Kramer agreed. "Don't worry, Pauline. You won't be here at Fort Alexander much longer."

"And I'll have a star in these shoulder straps for sure," Blackburn said.

"How wonderful," Pauline said with a slight smile. She left them and went back to the kitchen, removing her riding gloves in deep thought and contemplation.

CHAPTER 16

The double column of blue-clad troopers cantered across the prairie. The bright red and white guidons of each company whipped in the stiff wind that swept over the prairie country.

The two long lines of horsemen were made up of the entire First Squadron out of Fort Alexander. Companies A, B, C, and D with old Maj. Standish Scott and his staff entourage were out in the field because of telegraphed reports from posts in Texas. This late intelligence gave reliable indication that Lame Elk's band had turned north, headed for the Indian Territory or Kansas. The hostiles had committed murder and rapine in Texas, and were no doubt changing their raiding territory. They would have to pass through the patrol area along the Red River.

Among the Company C riders, looking alien but comfortable, the journalist Morris Kramer rode beside his old friend Gordon Blackburn. The newspaper man was dressed in a newly purchased buckskin jacket, riding breeches, and a pair of elegant boots. He carried a leather case containing his writing utensils over one shoulder. A jaunty pith helmet perched cockily on his head, and a bandanna, supplied by Blackburn, was tied around his neck to finish off his outfit.

In spite of his urban working life in the East, Kramer was an expert rider and handled the borrowed horse—an animal that belonged to an officer in the Third Squadron—with ease and dexterity. He looked over at his companion. "You never told me what you thought of those dispatches I wrote," Kramer said. "I saw you reading them last night by the campfire."

"They looked deucedly good, old man," Blackburn remarked. "In fact, I found them awe inspiring."

Kramer smiled. "I thought you would appreciate the numerous mentions of your name."

Blackburn laughed. "Of course! But, allow me, old friend, to compliment your flowery prose. Even your description of such a humdrum affair as preparing for patrol was filled with tension and excitement."

"Deep in this breast," Kramer said placing his hand on his chest, "beats the heart of a novelist. My editor has said I could take a dull old ladies' tea party and write it into a smashing, gala affair of elegance and gaiety."

"In that case, I am most anxious to see what you do with an Indian battle," Blackburn said.

"You just get me to one," Kramer said.

"I shall, don't worry. But you must remember who is to be at the center stage of this show."

"Of course. You realize, Gordon, that I need this as much as you. If I don't send back hair-raising stories of derring-do and heroic deeds, then I will be in deep trouble at my paper. I had a devil of a time talking my superiors into financing this excursion. It was necessary to promise them exciting copy filled with brave deeds and ferocious battles. So you can see, old man, that your build-up as an Indian fighter *sans egal* is as advantageous to me as it is to you. Both our careers are on the line here."

"We are at the mercy of the gods of war," Blackburn said. "So let us press on."

Kramer glanced around. He could see DuBose back a ways in the column on the other side of Pvt. Paddy McNally with the guidon and Trumpeter Benito Pullini. "There is an interesting fellow."

"Who is that?" Blackburn asked.

"Your sergeant—DuBose—a southerner from his manner of speaking," Kramer said. "His accent is remarkably like that of Pauline's."

Blackburn shrugged. "No surprise there. They are both from South Carolina, though Pauline's origins are in Georgia, I believe. As a matter of fact, DuBose was an officer in the rebel army."

"Really? There might be an interesting story there," Kramer said. "It would be intriguing to get the truth behind a former Confederate officer serving as a sergeant in the United States Cavalry. It could well be worth the trouble of getting an interview with him."

"Don't bother," Blackburn advised him. "I have already attempted several conversations with the fellow. The war evidently wiped him out financially, morally, and intellectually. Sometimes I even think him a bit stupid, but then I realize that he has stifled himself in the life he has chosen to lead. You would get only noncommittal grunts from the man."

"Ah, yes, I suppose it would be a bit of dreary dullness. He just can't make a success of himself in civilian life, so he takes the easy way in the army," Kramer said. "I've met a few officers like that too."

"Present company excepted?" Blackburn asked with a wink.

"Of course, old boy, of course!"

"Once I am back at the War Department, I'll show you success like you've never imagined," Blackburn said. "God! I must get away from this awful regiment."

"Pauline seems to be adapting rather well," Kramer remarked. "In fact, she's been downright chipper lately."

"Yes. I've noticed that myself. Of course she's an outwardly friendly person," Blackburn said. "Pauline can make herself fit in anywhere. She's evidently found good friends in the adjutant's and quartermaster's wives. The three are even talking of helping out Mrs. Druce over at the agency Indian school."

"Very good!" Kramer said. "I can put that in the stories too." He became thoughtful. "Let's see— dashing Indian fighter's compassionate wife strives to lead the foes' children onto the bright path of civilization."

"Sounds good to me," Blackburn said. "Though the little buggers make me think of that proverb which states, 'nits grow up to be lice.'"

Kramer laughed. "I'll leave that out, Gordon. We mustn't have the sob sisters back east thinking ill of you."

A flurry of shouting broke out along the column. The sound of several shots followed, and a trumpet blared out the signal for a flanking movement. A pounding of hooves came up from the rear. Major Scott appeared with his small staff. He leaned toward

Blackburn as he passed. "Stand fast in the column, Captain. Don't pay any attention to that trumpet."

Guy DuBose joined Blackburn and Kramer. "Sounds like some harassing fire up front, sir. One of the officers at the head of the column must have become excited and ordered a trumpeter to sound a field call."

"What is your assessment of the situation?" Blackburn asked.

"One of two things, sir. Possibly some of Lame Elk's warriors are having their version of fun," Guy explained. "There's too many of us to count coup, so they popped off some shots."

"What's the other possibility?" Kramer interjected.

"There is always the chance we'll be under attack," Guy answered. "Major Scott will find out up front. There's not much for us to do right now."

Another flurry of shots broke out to the left front, then more were heard to the immediate right. A horse whinnied and staggered out of the formation to collapse to the ground. Its rider, a veteran private, managed to leap clear in time. "God damn, boys, they shot my mount," he complained to his comrades.

Another trooper fell out of his saddle without a sound, crashing heavily to the grass. The kid beside him hollered out in a shrill voice, "Tommy's hit! Tommy's hit!"

By then Guy had surmised what was happening. "By sections, to the right flank, march! Draw pistols!"

The entire company wheeled into a double line facing in the proper direction.

"Pullini, sound *Charge!*"

The Italian grasped his trumpet and placed it to his

mouth. He played the urgent, rapid notes. The horses, as well-drilled as the men, leaped forward. Company C, with the exception of the dead man and the trooper who lost his horse, galloped toward a dip in the ground. Blackburn and Kramer followed, the newspaper man trying to observe all the activity going on around him.

Now several dismounted Indians could now be seen in the shallow gully they used for cover. The Chogolas fired methodically and carefully. The soldiers pressed, gaining speed, until they rode straight into the crowd of twenty Indians.

Guy, in the lead, fired his pistol into the face of one warrior, but another used his lance to sweep the sergeant from the saddle. Guy hit painfully on his back, losing the grip on his pistol. He instinctively sat up in time to see the company gallop on out of the depression. He was left all alone among the hostiles until the troopers could be turned around and brought back.

The Chogola, yelling loudly, stabbed at Guy with the lance. Guy rolled to the side as the point sliced into the earth beside him. Damning the pain in his back, he got to his feet and faced his adversary. The Indian began a series of feints, faking for different parts of Guy's body. The warrior's friends, who had been enjoying the fun, now had to turn and deal with the company that had halted and reformed.

Guy dodged and ducked while the lance head darted at him. There was a slash at his neck, a fake toward his genitals, then a genuine attack at his abdomen. Guy parried with his left hand, knocking the shaft up and away. At the same time he grabbed the lance with his right, pivoting violently until his back was to the Indian. The warrior kicked him in the rear of the legs, making Guy turn around to face him. Both men, grimacing in physical effort and hatred, hung on to the primitive weapon.

Thoughts of finally finding Pauline and perhaps losing her because of being killed by the Indian infuriated the soldier. "God—damn—you," Guy hissed through tightly clenched teeth as he pulled and tugged. "You—son—of—a—bitch!"

The Chogola, uttering only grunts and moans, shook furiously as he tried to pull the weapon out of Guy's strong grip. Zinging shots and ricochets abruptly broke on the scene, as did the sound of many hooves rapidly approaching. Now both combatants, regardless of being soldier or Indian, were in danger of Company C's bullets on the return charge.

When Pullini's blaring trumpet was so loud it almost drowned out the sound of the shooting, both Guy and the Indian let loose of the lance and scrambled away in opposite directions to safety. Guy had run a few yards when a horse drew up beside him.

"Would ye care fer a ride, Sargint?" Donovan asked slipping his left boot from the stirrup.

"Thank you most kindly," Guy said putting his own foot in before hauling himself aboard.

They rode fast to catch up with the rest of the company. They caught up with the others when Blackburn, who had taken command, brought them to a halt. "Company!" he hollered. "Wheel about, march!" But before he could order another charge, the sound of *Officers Call* came from the center of the scattered column. "Stand fast!" He noted that Guy, who had slid off the rump of Donovan's horse, was dismounted. The captain yelled over to Sergeant Harry Tate. "Take over the company until my return."

"Yes, sir!" Harry responded. "Reholster yore pistols and draw them carbines!"

The company—men and horses both—were still excited after the action. They milled about restlessly. Guy called over to Privates Tim Donovan and Benny Horn. "Ride over past the ambush site and fetch my mount. But if he's headed outward, forget it. And check the area where the Indians were located. My pistol is there somewhere."

The two, anxious to do something, galloped happily away to the job. Morris Kramer, who had simply ridden empty-handed through the action, walked his horse over to Guy. "That was quite a situation you were in, Sergeant."

Guy reached back and rubbed his sore back. His arms also ached with the effort of tugging on the lance. "I've had more enjoyable moments," he said.

"I'd like to write that up, if you don't mind," Kramer said. "Care to make a descriptive statement for me?"

Guy shrugged. "Did you see what happened?"

"Yes."

"Then there is nothing I can add to it." Guy turned away and watched Donovan and Horn return with his horse.

Donovan rode up and handed the reins over. "We couldn't find yer pistol, Sargint. Them heathens musta took it wit'em."

Guy nodded. "That'll mean a mountain of paperwork for the quartermaster." He swung up into his saddle glad to be back aboard his horse. "But thanks for trying."

Horn had grown pensive. "Say, Donovan. It looks like we could get killed out here."

"That we could, young Benny Horn," Donovan answered. "Don't tell me ye're gittin' religion now, are ye?"

"No, nothing like that. But I'd sure like to clear up something, if you don't mind," Horn said. "It's really been bothering me and I'd feel better getting it off my chest."

Donovan was curious. "Sure now, young soljer, and ye sound like ye've got a guilty conscience. If ye got somethin' to say to me, just come on out wit' it."

"Do you remember the night you got drunk at the sutler's store and got throwed in the guard house?"

"A bit of it, yeah," Donovan answered with a grin.

"Well, I'm the one that bashed you on the head with my carbine," Horn said almost fearfully. "I wanted to clear that up."

Donovan burst out into Irish laughter. "And is that botherin' ye, young soljer?"

"Will you forgive me, Donovan?" Horn asked. "Maybe you'd like to punch me, huh? I'll let you. I deserve it."

"I'll not be givin' ye a clout to the jaw. Ye were only doin' yer duty. So ye're forgiven," Donovan said. "And ye're as good a comrade as this ol' soljer has ever knowed."

"Thank you, Donovan," Horn said relieved. "I'm proud to be your friend."

"Hey, Private Donovan," McNally hollered over to

him. "There's somethin' I want to clear up too."

Donovan scowled. "And what's that, Private McNally?"

"I'm wishin' I was the one what did bash you that night, Private Donovan," McNally said.

"I'll see ye behind the barracks first chance then, Private McNally," Donovan growled. "And ye can bet I'll—"

He was interrupted by the arrival of Captain Blackburn. The officer noted that Guy was remounted. "We're heading back to Fort Alexander," he announced loudly to the company. "We're being relieved by the Second Squadron who will continue the chase. Take charge, Sergeant DuBose."

"Yes, sir."

The captain and Kramer joined up to head the column. Blackburn was dejected, "Tough luck. What happened?"

"The Second Squadron commander had complained to the colonel that we were getting all the glory," Blackburn said. "So we have been pulled out of the field to guard the garrison."

"Don't worry," Kramer said. "I've got plenty of good copy here. Let's see—'Brave Captain Blackburn leads thundering charge and smashes hostile Indian attack.'"

"Well," Blackburn said sighing. "It's a start."

"Form a column of sections!" Guy DuBose shouted back at the company. "March!"

Pvt. Paddy McNally with the guidon, accompanied by Trumpeter Pullini, rode to their proper positions next to the company commander.

CHAPTER 17

The Indian girls, all students of Netta Druce at the Red River Agency School, sat at their places in absolute stillness. The children, with their little hands clasped together on the desk tops, ranged in age from five to twelve years. The contrast between the school room and the civilized furniture in it with the primitiveness of the small students' attire of buckskin dresses and beaded moccasins was stark, yet had a certain charm at the same time.

The officers' ladies, Pauline Blackburn, Minnie Robertson, and Violet Harris, beamed at the little girls from where they sat at a table especially placed in the front of the room for them. They had all dressed in their finest dresses as if making Church Call with their husbands. Pauline's more fashionable finery was obvious even to the untrained eyes of the Indian children.

Sgt. Guy DuBose, once again acting as an escort, stood by the door at the back of the room. He wanted to take this unique opportunity to fill his eyes with the uninterrupted sight of Pauline. But Mrs. Robertson and Mrs. Harris glanced at him too frequently.

The teacher wasted no time in beginning her program. "Ladies," Netta said addressing them in a formal manner with her own hands folded in front. "I am most happy and pleased to welcome you to the Red River Agency School. This is a government-sponsored institution staffed by the Christian Pacification Society. The cost of operation is borne by both groups. The money from our society comes from generous donations by the Christian brethren who are members. That amount accounts for more than half our funds, so we like to think of our effort here as more of a philanthropic enterprise than an official one."

Pauline Blackburn raised her hand. "Excuse me, please, Mrs. Druce. I noticed that the class is made up of all girls. Is there another for the Indian boys?"

"Alas, no," Netta sadly replied. "The culture of the Chogola Comanches, indeed of all the Plains Indians, does not permit their young males to participate in such activities. I must confess that we must pay even the families of these little girls with trinkets and other items from the agency store. Without these well-intentioned bribes, I fear the Indian fathers and mothers would never send their daughters to us. But it is a start, and we thank the Good Lord for even this rather disappointing beginning."

Guy noticed that the Chogola girls had adapted rather well into the learning environment. He also could well understand why none of their brothers attended. No self-respecting Comanche boy would tolerate having to sit inside a stuffy room learning lessons he considered useless and feminine. Knowing how to read did not help one hunt buffalo, make weapons, or learn the powerful medicine necessary to be a full-fledged male member of the tribe. Their culture was based on warfare pure and simple. The warriors' entire reason for existing was to hunt, fight, and plunder. Guy knew from first hand experience that they were experts at all those dangerous activities.

"Our primary concern, of course," Netta continued, "is the saving of their souls. The first lessons here are those of the Holy Gospel, and we make it a part of every lesson whenever possible. As a demonstration of this I shall ask Rebecca, Mary, and Rachel to sing for us. I only wish we had a piano to accompany them, but I am sure you will agree that their sweet voices more than make up for the lack of musical instruments." As the little girls dutifully got out of their seats and went to a place in front of the class, Netta explained, "I have given them Christian names to replace those of their tribe. I consider this a big step toward their eventual conversion. When they accept baptism, they will be ready with proper names that God can understand." She turned to the girls. "The ladies are ready to hear your song."

The little trio of six to eight-year-olds launched into *Jesus Loves Me*. They sang in English, yet in the tremor of their small voices Guy could recognize the tonal values used by the Indian women in their songs of triumph and mourning after a war party returned to camp. He wondered if Netta Druce and her husband understood how deeply rooted the Indians' own religious beliefs were imbedded in their souls.

When the song finished, the girls smiled in open pride at this display of their accomplishment. Pauline,

Minnie, and Violet, completely charmed by the singing, applauded and cooed as the girls returned to their seats.

This was followed by several recitations of lessons and poetry. The final performance, the *piece de resistance,* was the entire class standing up to sing the *Battle Hymn of the Republic.* The conclusion of this rousing song brought the officers' ladies to their feet. They clapped heartily as both teacher and students took their bows.

Netta sat her students down. "Ruth, will you please take charge of the class while we are gone?"

A beautiful Indian girl of twelve years stood up and walked to the front. She was sensuous even at that age, her buckskin dress swaying with her graceful gait. "Yes, Mrs. Druce."

Guy knew some handsome young warrior would seduce her away from the white people's way in another couple of summers. If that likely event didn't happen, the powerful medicine of her culture would cause the young Chogola girl to let go of the white man's hand and return to the road of her people.

But Netta Druce didn't seem to notice. "Have the class practice the alphabet until it is time for school to end for the day. It is only for another half hour."

The Chogola girl named Ruth looked up at the clock.

Netta glanced at the women. "I have taught her to tell time." She turned her attention back to the girl. "Do you understand, Ruth?"

"Yes, Mrs. Druce."

Netta turned to the three women. "Please come with me. I would like to show you the rest of the agency. I hope not to sound immodest, but my husband and I are very proud of our accomplishments here."

"Dear me!" Minnie Robertson exclaimed. "Are we going among the teepees?"

"Oh, no," Netta said. "My husband would not permit it. He says there are things there that—well, excuse me!—but there are things and activities in a primitive Indian camp that ladies shouldn't see."

"What things?" Violet Harris asked.

"Violet!" Pauline exclaimed. "You are so wicked!"

"Oh, for heaven's sake!" Minnie exclaimed. "Even I've been among the lodges. The worst thing one might see is a woman nursing her child."

"Outside?" Pauline asked incredulously.

"Yes, my dear," Minnie said. "Outside."

Netta led the way to the door. They walked past Guy with Pauline trailing. As he opened the door and ushered them through to the outside, he and Pauline gave each other a subtle but meaningful look.

"I'll show you our store," Netta said. "The goods are not as nice as those at the sutler's, and certainly not as elegant as those in town shops, but they do quite well for our Indian brethren."

They walked across the yard to the building. Guy, with Pauline to his direct front, brought up the rear. After entering, they stood off to the far side of the counter while Netta showed some blankets, metal pots, and simple tools. Guy moved his hand forward and touched Pauline's arm. She stepped a bit closer, keeping her eye on Netta.

Then her hand slipped into Guy's.

It was wonderful! She could feel the warmth of his flesh against hers. The sensation flooding her memory

191

anew of evening strolls and country balls on the Berger Plantation. But she was no longer a virgin, and the touch of the man she loved carried her thoughts past innocent courtship to passionate lovemaking of the sweetest kind. Pauline wanted Guy more than she ever had in the past. Her need for him was womanly and physically demanding, yet the emotional side of her love had matured and intensified also.

Guy's own sensations of love melted away the bitterness that once only alcohol could dull. He didn't give a damn about anything except having Pauline as his own. It was a desire he knew would have to be satisfied. At that particular point, Guy DuBose was ready to take on whatever sort of hell would descend on him if he made a move to covet an officer's wife. The only thing that held him back was not wanting any of the bitter wrath to hurt Pauline. Guy knew the situation would have to be carefully and thoroughly planned out. He had eight months left to serve in the army. There was nothing he could safely do until he received his discharge.

Netta interrupted the lovers' thoughts as she walked toward the door. "Now I'll show you our two milk cows," she said. "Palmer originally came here with five, but one was struck ill and died. The other two, I am afraid to say, were killed and butchered by the Chogolas—the very people the unfortunate animals were supposed to serve."

"Ungrateful wretches!" Minnie Robertson exclaimed.

"Indeed," Violet agreed.

Guy recalled that the cows were killed when a winter undershipment of government beef ran out. The

Chogolas, at that low point in an extremely bitter winter, faced starvation. As the ladies moved away, he had to let Pauline slip out of his hand.

The walk to the barn was a short one. The building, with numerous stalls for animals, was long and dark. Palmer Druce was inside working with a pitchfork as he hurled hay into the feeding troughs of the dairy cattle. A Chogola man, who had taken heavily to civilization's whiskey, worked with him. The Indian had even adopted regular clothing though he kept his hair long and braided. He was a common sight at Fort Alexander, proving an example of how harmful the White Man's Road could be for an Indian bred to warring and hunting.

"Good morning, ladies," Palmer Druce greeted. "Come and look at my beauties."

The two cows, munching contentedly, lazily swung their heads to observe the unusual sight of the women in the barn. The guests made appropriate complimentary remarks which set Palmer to talking about his grandiose plans for the barn. "I'll soon have this place fully stocked with every useful animal there is. Why I'll have plough horses, mules, cows, goats, and sheep. I fully intend to have the Red River Agency operating without a red cent from the Federal government. There is every chance that we might even become self-supporting."

"Most admirable," Pauline said.

"Go on and look around," Palmer said. "You'll be able to see that we're ready to take on more than the Chogolas if the need arises. There are the other tribes of Comanches and even the Kiowas in this area. Eventually all will have to be settled someplace. I believe the Red River Agency is the best location."

The agent was not so much interested in favorably impressing the ladies themselves as he was having them return to their husbands with glowing accounts on how the agency was being run. There had been several run-ins with the military bureaucracy. If the army at Fort Alexander was favorably impressed, their official reports would reflect it.

Minnie and Violet walked forward to look into the stalls and tool rooms in that part of the barn. Pauline gave Guy a meaningful look, then walked slowly and deliberately in the opposite direction. Guy shot a quick look at Netta. She had been drawn into an earnest conversation of some sort with Palmer. Guy, turning slowly, ambled off in the direction that Pauline had taken.

They met in an empty stall that had heavy draft horse harnesses hanging over the entrance. Pauline went into his arms and lifted her face to his. For the first time in twelve years, Guy pressed his lips against those of his true love. She responded with quick breaths, grasping him hard and holding him, tears coming to her eyes. They parted reluctantly, but immediately kissed again. This time without so much urgency, but with more softness.

"I love you with all my heart, Pauline," Guy whispered huskily.

"And I am yours, darling," she said. She sighed, remembering her true status of being wed to Gordon Blackburn. "I want to be yours."

"I'll work it out," he promised.

"I must get back," Pauline said hearing the other women's aimless wandering getting closer.

"I'll wait a few moments," Guy said. "Go ahead." He stood behind the horse tackle, giving her a chance to join the others. After a few moments, he stepped out and, unnoticed by them, rejoined the group.

In the next stall, where she had been gathering eggs from the nests of the hens who roosted in the barn, Inez continued to kneel behind the cover of the wooden wall. Only after the others had left, did she walk out with her basket of eggs.

Netta made her goodbys to her visitors. Guy helped the ladies up into the side saddles, then mounted his own horse. At that time the Indian girls trooped out of the schoolhouse and headed back for the Chogola camp. All waved at the visitors. The ladies replied in kind. After more cordial farewells to Netta, the small group rode out of the agency yard, turning south for the river ford.

Netta walked back toward the house and noticed Inez standing on the porch. She frowned at the Mexican girl. "What are you doing there?"

"I just picked up some eggs, *Señora*," Inez said.

"Did you finish your chores in the front of the house?"

"No," Inez answered.

Netta's expression showed her displeasure. "Then why, pray tell me, did you go gathering eggs?"

Inez shrugged. "Because I wanted to. I don't like working in the house so much. I cannot breathe there."

"You spent too much time in that Indian camp for your own good," Netta said. "It seems we shall have to work much harder to recivilize you. Then you will be more comfortable indoors." She paused. "Or would you rather return to the Chogolas?"

195

"That is a terrible thing to say!" Inez snapped. She had spent almost three years of being raped nightly by an Indian warrior who had chosen her to be his woman.

"Well? Do you?" Netta pressed. "I've not been satisfied with you, Inez. You are obstinate and lazy."

"So! You give me back to the *indios,* eh? That is good of you," Inez said. She was infuriated by this casual attitude toward the hell she had endured. "I thought you were—were—*cristiana.*"

Netta understood the Spanish. "Of course I am a Christian, you wicked girl, and I am doing my best to bring you into our fold."

"I was not a Chogola's woman by choice. I have always been *catolica,*" Inez said. "So I am already belonging."

"You are a sinner!"

"You are the sinner," Inez said. She smirked and tossed her head. "You dream of the sergeant, no? Is that not as bad as being in bed with him? That is what you really want I think."

"You shut your mouth!" Netta said furiously.

"Well, I tell you something," Inez said. "You are not woman enough for him. I see him kissing the other lady in the barn."

Netta was so surprised she could not respond.

Inez leaned toward her. "I saw the Sergeant DuBose kiss the new lady in the barn. They were in the stall next to where I pick up the eggs. They were hot—*hot* with passion for each other." She laughed. "I think they make love the first chance they get."

Netta trembled with hurtful anger, but she recovered enough to speak. "Get in the house and tend to your

196

chores!" she said. She turned and walked back to the empty schoolhouse. She went up to her desk at the front and sat down in the chair behind it.

The one thing that kept life bearable for her was the secret fantasy romance with Sergeant DuBose. Her mind continued to be filled with pictures of him carrying her away to some phantom love den. During the warming weather, with more and more exposure to him during frequent visits by troops to the agency, her dream world had expanded until all her thoughts were consumed with the illusory love affair.

As long as he remained unattached, that mental world could whirl on with some sense of reality—even hope. Now all that had been dashed.

Netta knew that the young Mexican woman was speaking the truth. She had no doubts that the handsome sergeant had finally attracted someone— even a married officer's wife—to his arms. Even though it was inevitable, it cut her as deep as if she were truly a woman scorned. Now, alone and miserable, Netta wept with the grief the loneliness of her life had burdened her with.

"It isn't fair!" she cried to herself. "I hate him! And I hate her! It isn't fair!"

CHAPTER 18

The officers' room at the sutler's store was the closest thing to a gentlemen's club that Fort Alexander had to offer. On Thursday nights the entire building was turned over to the rankers for weekly get-togethers. With the enlisted men out of the way, their superiors were able to relax and be themselves.

The soldiers, rather than being resentful, understood this need for diversion among the staff and commanders. The only complaint they had was about bad-tempered officers on Friday mornings who showed up for duty suffering visible ill-effects from the previous evening's drinking.

Although there was no possibility for any real wickedness such as the troops had with the numerous "hog ranches" that showed up for brief stints at the edge of the post, the officers could at least unbutton their tunics and enjoy indulging in a few drinks in the company of their peers.

The idea had been Colonel Gatley's. During a short period as a subaltern he had been posted to the

American embassy in London. His duties dictated much socializing with British officers. He found their officers messes and the masculine-oriented socializing there an enjoyable feature. The gatherings in the crude sutler's store on this isolated post were the closest thing he had now. But the colonel was determined to at least create the proper gentlemanly atmosphere.

Like the more elegant British events, Fort Alexander's officers mess did not really begin until the senior officers arrived in the shank of the evening. The less formal side of the occasion began promptly after Retreat, when the subalterns first arrived at the sutler's store. The job of these lieutenants was to make sure the correct liquor and refreshments were in generous supply, and that the room was properly arranged. Mr. Dawkins, the sutler, was on hand to make sure that these juniors had all they deemed necessary. All this was done while their superiors stopped at home to relax and visit with their wives, who had spent the day tending to their own part of army life amid the genteel clutter and clatter of officers row.

After the lieutenants had seen to these preliminary tasks, the next group of officers to arrive were the captains. With the exception of the younger Blackburn, most of these men were in their late forties. They made a cursory inspection of the lieutenants' efforts. They always found something that needed fixing or correcting, so Mr. Dawkins would reappear to set things right. Once all that was settled, the captains waited with the subalterns until the majors arrived. Those gentlemen did nothing but go to their favorite seats and settle down to have Dawkins serve them. Once that was done, enough time elapsed for everyone present to enjoy a drink. Then, as it had become the custom, Dawkins withdrew from the scene and every gentleman served himself.

Finally, to make the gathering official, the colonel, accompanied by the adjutant and the quartermaster, came through the door. It was a freshly implemented regimental tradition that the lowest ranking second lieutenant bawl out a resounding, "Tin hut!" At that time the entire room snapped to attention, and the commanding officer had the floor until he relinquished it to the more festive aspects of the evening.

The night after the three officers' wives' trip to the Red River Agency, Colonel Gatley was particularly affable. He put the men at ease and invited them to take their seats.

"We all know we have a guest," he said. "But I would like to make special mention of the occasion and extend an official welcome to the distinguished journalist Mr. Morris Kramer of the *Washington Daily Chronicle.*"

Kramer, taking his cue, stood up. He had been allowed to move into one of the empty subaltern billets, so he no longer shared the Blackburn quarters. "Thank you, Colonel Gatley. I appreciate the kindness that the officers of regiment have extended me in the invitation to join them here tonight. You've all made me feel welcome here at Fort Alexander as well as in the field. Thank you. Thank you all very much."

Gatley chuckled. "Of course, Mr. Kramer, we will expect your stories to impress the public back east that our gallant regiment is winning the west for the United States and civilization."

The other officers responded properly with laughter

at the colonel's humor. But there was a very serious side to that part of the reporter's relationship with Fort Alexander. Normally, a newspaper man would have to fight snarled red tape to gain such free and nearly unlimited access to an army post. But both the commanding general of the Military Department of Texas and Colonel Gatley recognized that a sympathetic slant in news dispatches could very well lead to certain advantages. Officers, whose names appeared as troop commanders linked to victories, could expect a favorable response from a sensitive War Department who needed some real heroes to parade before congress and the American people. Gatley's motives were more unselfish. He hoped the adjutant general's department would see that a larger share of the cavalry recruits sent to Jefferson Barracks, Missouri would be transferred to his badly understrength regiment. And his officer cadre could use a few recent West Point graduates too.

Blackburn's role in Kramer's presence was not lost on the participants either. Gatley knew that the dark, unhappy captain was calling in a favor or two. No doubt he would be the center of Kramer's articles in the *Daily Chronicle,* but at least there should be enough glory to spill over on the others too.

"Gentlemen," the colonel said. "I have a most important announcement to make before we settle down to the social side of this evening's gathering. A telegram has recently arrived from Fort Riley, Kansas, which tells us that our old nemesis—and neighborhood bully—Lame Elk seems to be heading back in our direction."

There was a cheer from the officers.

Gatley smiled. "We don't get the long, war-winning

expeditions to the field that the larger commands enjoy." He looked meaningfully at Kramer. "Since our regiment is barely at half-strength, we must content ourselves with short, local patrols." He paused, then raised his voice. "But we shall take the utmost advantage of these small opportunities. It is my fervent hope that this regiment is the one that smashes Lame Elk and his band and leads them, limping and moaning, back to the Red River Agency where they belong!"

Another chorus of lusty cheers shook the room.

Now the commander shamelessly toadied up to a lower-ranking officer. "I am going to put Captain Blackburn and his gallant men of C Company at the forefront of this latest action. I shall send them out as point unit, to make the first contact with the hostiles. The remainder of the three squadrons will follow, with the exception of those troops detailed for post guard, of course."

The response was not so vocal at that point. Most of the officers glanced over at the beaming Blackburn with expressions close to sneers. They also realized his and Kramer's relationship, and knew the captain was pulling out all stops to get back to a War Department desk in Washington City.

"Reveille and all the daily service will be one hour earlier tomorrow," Colonel Gatley said. "I will expect Captain Blackburn to sally forth at no later than seven o'clock in the morning. The departure of the remainder of the regiment will be announced tomorrow." He turned to his staff. "Both Lieutenant Harris and Lieutenant Robertson have announcements."

Harris, the adjutant, as per custom went first. "Since

the first sergeants will, of course, not accompany their units to the field, I will hold First Sergeants Call instead of the sergeant major. It will be at the regular time and I advise you to pass on any pertinent information or questions you have to those N.C.O.s. I will handle whatever business is discussed while you are on patrol. Thank you."

The quartermaster Lieutenant Robertson was just as brief. "Ammunition and rations will be issued to those troops going to the field right after Reveille. Company C will be first, then Second Squadron, First Squadron, and the Third lastly."

"That is it, gentlemen," Colonel Gatley said. "Now let's relax a bit and imbibe some well deserved drinks. But remember! You know your own tolerance both in getting home tonight and sitting in a saddle under the hot sun tomorrow."

The same lieutenant who had ordered the room to attention at the colonel's appearance once more bellowed the command.

"Carry on, gentlemen," Gatley said going to his own table with his staff following. That was the signal that the purely social side of the evening had begun.

Blackburn and Kramer sat alone at a table. None of the other officers deigned to join them. Even the affable Kramer could not attract more than passing greetings as the men settled down to friendly conversations and to compare the gossip they had garnered from their wives.

Blackburn, with a tall bottle of whiskey in front of him, poured a stiff drink into a tumbler. These glasses, bought by the officers out of the mess fund, were only for Thursday nights. Any other drinking activity at the sutler's store was done in government issue tin cups that Dawkins had to purchase from the quartermaster out of his profits.

Kramer raised his glass. "Give us a toast, Gordon."

Blackburn smiled. "That's easy, old boy." He raised his tumbler and tapped it against Kramer's. "To Washington City."

"To Washington City," Kramer said.

"And the good life awaiting me there," Blackburn added.

"Amen," Kramer tacked on with a smile.

"How many stories have you sent back?"

"Five total," Kramer answered. "Three went out together today. I wish there was a regular run to Dahlquart. That's the nearest telegraph station."

"What we need," Blackburn said finishing off the drink, "is a signal corps detachment to be assigned to Fort Alexander."

"It wouldn't do us any good," Kramer said. "You'll be long gone before that."

Blackburn laughed. "You bet I will!" He poured himself another drink, suddenly remembering Captain Dan Wayne. "You know, an officer here once said I'd become a hard drinker if I stayed very long." He took a stiff gulp. "And he was right. My God in heaven, how he was right!"

"Well, I'm sure we can get some great copy out of tomorrow's outing," Kramer said. "I just hope we can do as the colonel hoped and force that Lame Elk back to the agency."

"What if he won't go and we simply wipe out the son of a bitch?" Blackburn asked. Not used to heavy drinking, the whiskey was quickly going to his head.

Kramer was thoughtful for a moment. "Yes! That would be better. I could write up how you ended a murderous threat out on the frontier for once and all."

Blackburn grinned, his voice a bit slurred. "Y'know, Morris. If you're not careful, you're going to make a gen'ral outta me."

"Well, old son, if I do and you get to high places in the War Department, don't forget who got you there when there is important and earth-shaking news in the offing, eh?"

"Don't you worry a bit 'bout that," Blackburn said. He drank some more, the rush of intoxication making him giddy.

The other officers circulated freely in this informal Officers Call. Before long the main attraction of the evening began—poker. Three tables were finally set up to accommodate everybody, and the dealing began. The stakes weren't high, but the playing was intense as the atmosphere grew smokier and quieter when the hum of masculine voices was reduced to making and calling bets before the cards were shown.

As Blackburn drank his passions grew. He thought of his wife back in the quarters all alone now that Kramer had moved out. Not a sexually-driven man, his bouts of passionate desire were infrequent and short-lived. But when upon him they were intense. After a couple of hours, his need was so great that he decided to excuse himself.

"Morris, old man, I must go to the field t'morrow, y'know?"

"That's right. And I am going with you."

"E'zacley," Blackburn said. "So I'm going home and go to sleep. G'night."

206

"Good night, Gordon."

Blackburn staggered out into the cooler night air. It cleared his head enough to make it easier for him to make his way out of the area and go the short distance to Officers Row without staggering too much. He didn't want any of the enlisted men to see him drunk. The captain didn't know that the sight of officers stumbling homeward on Thursday nights was such a normal thing that most of the soldiers didn't give it much thought one way or the other.

He went past the subaltern's quarters and was almost at his own when a shadowy figure stepped out from the shadows. It was an Indian. Blackburn was startled until he noticed the man was dressed in a shirt and trousers. He recognized the Chogola as the harmless drunkard who hung around the post during times he wasn't working with Palmer Druce at the agency.

"You Cap'n Blackburn?"

Blackburn grinned crookedly. "Sure. Whattayou want, you Indian?"

"I got paper for you," the Chogola said. He shoved a folded document at him. "It from the Druce woman."

"What'n hell does she want?"

"I got paper for you."

"I asked you a question, Indian."

The man stuck to the basic intent of his errand. "This paper is for you. I give it to you. Take it."

"I shall," Blackburn said grasping the note and shoving it in his pocket. He waved at the Indian, then went on to his door. When he stepped inside he could see that Pauline had already gone to bed. He liked waking her up with his demands. She was always warm and already undressed beneath her nightgown.

He remembered what the Chogola had given him. Blackburn pulled it out of his pocket and unfolded the missive. The lantern in the living room was turned low and he had to get close to read it. The first few words swept away the intoxication like a dash of ice cold water. He shook his head, then turned the lamp up to its brightest illumination. Blackburn read it again slower, each word sinking into his brain.

"Pauline!" he roared in anger. Picking up the lantern, he charged through the curtains into the bedroom.

Pauline, her eyes opened wide with fright, sat up in bed, grasping the covers close to her. "Gordon? What in the world is the matter?"

"You read this God damned note!" he demanded. "Now why would Mrs. Druce write such a thing?"

Pauline rubbed her eyes and took the paper. She read slowly, then set it down in her lap.

"Well? Say something," Blackburn said. "Tell me it is a pack of lies. Surely you did not embrace and kiss that enlisted swine DuBose!"

"I should have told you," she said. "It all goes so far back in time now. I'm so sorry, Gordon."

"You had a cheap rendezvous with a common soldier in the Druce barn?" he asked in angry amazement.

"It wasn't like that at all," Pauline said softly. "Guy DuBose and I were engaged to be married before the war. I thought he was dead. A dear boy who was mortally wounded told me that he'd seen him die at Gettysburg." She looked up at him. "You can imagine my shock when I arrived here and—"

"Damn *your* shock, you harlot! Have you no

thoughts of me?"

"Of course, Gordon, of course," Pauline said sorrowfully. "Please don't call me names. I can't help what happened."

Gordon was speechless for a few moments as the liquor's effect now completely left him. He was cold and calculating. "I don't give a damn about some long-ago engagement. It is not going to be the cause of my becoming a public cuckold. A charge of rape should settle that rebel son of a bitch," he said.

"Gordon," Pauline said with renewed strength in her voice. "I shall deny it."

"Would you shame me?"

She was glad it had come out into the home. "I cannot continue as your wife, Gordon. I do not want to."

"To hell with what you want or not want," Blackburn said. "I am not giving you a divorce so you can run off with some sergeant. I am doing everything possible to re-establish myself in the army's highest cadre. Such a scandal would ruin my career for good. So I'll decide what happens from this point on." He reached down and grabbed her arm. "Don't you dare mention this to a soul, do you hear?"

"Let go, Gordon. That is very painful," she said wincing.

"You stay quiet about this shameful episode, or I'll kill you!"

The cold, furious tone in his voice was under such control that Pauline had never been so frightened in her life.

CHAPTER 19

Pvt. Tim Donovan knelt down and carefully studied the marks on the ground for several long moments. After more detailed scrutiny, he walked out a few yards before returning to the original position. He did this in several directions before he finally reported to Captain Gordon Blackburn. The officer waited with the journalist Morris Kramer back at the main column of Company C.

Donovan, his horse's reins in his hands, looked up at the commanding officer. "Sir, them Injuns is split up into three groups," the old soldier reported. "They went due south, southeast and southwest."

"Thank you, Private Donovan," Blackburn said. "You may rejoin your section." He gestured to Kramer. "Well, Morris, it appears that I have a tactical decision to make."

"It certainly does, Gordon," Kramer said.

Blackburn motioned back to Guy DuBose to come forward and join him. Guy left his post behind Trumpeter Pullini and Private McNally. "Yes, sir?"

"Sergeant, did you hear Donovan's report?"

"Yes, sir."

"I would appreciate your professional opinion on the situation, Sergeant DuBose."

Guy had been leery of Blackburn since they'd ridden out of Fort Alexander earlier that morning. The captain had been aloof yet had spoken to him in almost friendly tones from time to time during the long ride. "Sir," Guy said. "Since we are north of the Red River Agency and deep into Indian Territory, I perceive but three possibilities in Lame Elk's actions. He could be leading us into an ambush. On the other hand, he might be circling around to hit us from different sides, or he feels that splitting up his band will force us to do the same thing. That would facilitate his escape."

"Any other possible situations, Sergeant?"

"Yes, sir," Guy answered. "They have women and children with them. Perhaps they are trying to get them away to safety. The warriors may even be leading their families back to the Red River Agency."

"Did you get all that down, Morris?"

Kramer, scribbling in a notepad, nodded. "I certainly did."

"How interesting," Blackburn said. He turned to Harry Tate sitting his horse not far away. "Did you hear Sergeant DuBose's evaluation of the situation?"

"Yes, sir," Tate answered.

Blackburn smiled. "How did your fellow N.C.O. impress you, Sergeant?"

Tate felt uneasy. He also had noticed Blackburn's unusual behavior. "I got a lotta faith in Sergeant DuBose, sir. If he's ever wrong it ain't very often."

Blackburn looked back at Guy. "What a compliment—though a bit lefthanded—from a fellow professional, Sergeant. You must be flattered. I imagine that Morris will put that in his article."

"It's just what the readers want to see," Kramer answered with a wink at Guy DuBose. "Before I'm done, you cavalry troopers will be the talk of the eastern seaboard."

Guy said nothing.

Blackburn pointed to the ground. "One of those trails is marked so well that it can be followed easily on horseback."

Tate interrupted. "That'd be the one Lame Elk wants us to foller, sir."

"The most dangerous then?" Blackburn asked. "Because it could be a trap."

"Yes, sir," Tate answered.

"Then we must put our best man on it," Blackburn said. "Sergeant DuBose, scout that track until you come into physical contact with those Indians making it."

"Yes, sir," Guy replied. "But the number of hostiles involved will badly outnumber a section of troops."

"Section? Section?" Blackburn asked with a smile. "Why, Sergeant DuBose! Who said anything about a section? I want you to go alone. It's too dangerous except for a tried-and-true old Indian fighting soldier like yourself."

"Sir!" Harry Tate shouted. "He wouldn't stand a chance a'tall!"

Blackburn's smile faded and he spoke to Guy in deliberate tones, glaring straight into the N.C.O.'s face. "I am ordering you to follow that trail until you find the hostiles who created it, Sergeant. And I am ordering

213

you to do it alone."

"Yes, sir."

Blackburn spoke again to Kramer. "Be kind, Morris. Write that he volunteered for the patrol. It will make him sound braver and more dedicated."

At that precise moment Guy realized that Blackburn had found out about Pauline and him. He also now knew that his life was practically worthless in the field as long as he was under the captain's control. The best thing to do was face the situation straight on. Perhaps Blackburn would back down. "Sir," Guy said. "I volunteer for the patrol."

"Guy! Yo're crazy!" Harry Tate shouted. "Lame Elk's gonna roast you alive!"

Morris Kramer was growing confused. "I don't understand exactly what the situation is."

"It is simple, Morris," Blackburn said. "We have a dangerous mission and Sergeant DuBose has bravely volunteered for it." The captain was going to play his slanted game to the hilt.

Guy reached in his tunic and pulled out a cigar. He bit off the end. "Kramer," he said. "Have you got that name right? It's spelled D-U-B-O-S-E. The D and B are capitalized."

"Right," Morris replied.

"Where will I find the company when I return, sir?" Guy asked Blackburn as he lit the stogie.

"That's easy, Sergeant," Blackburn said pointing at the ground. "Somewhere along one of these two other trails."

"Yes, sir. Thank you, sir," Guy said. "By your leave, I'll begin the scout."

"Carry on, Sergeant."

214

Guy nodded a curt farewell to Harry Tate, then kicked his horse in the flanks and galloped away from the column. He rode fast along the Chogola trail until he topped a gentle rise and dropped down to more level ground. Only then did Guy ease back on the reins to slow the horse. He also pulled his Springfield carbine from its saddleboot and opened the flap of his holster to make the pistol more accessible. The plan, in case he confronted hostile warriors, was to fire one distant, well-aimed shot with the single-shot long arm. After that he would rely on the Remington for the close-in work.

The terrain that stretched out before him was flat and undulating with deep prairie grass. Individual trees, stark and alone, dotted the landscapes at far intervals. It was an easy place for a dismounted man to hide, but one on horseback was as visible as those infrequent redbuds and cottonwoods.

At one point Guy could see far enough ahead to determine which direction the trail had headed. He turned at a right angle, going almost a full mile away before turning back to ride parallel to the track until he reached a point where he was forced to ride back to find it again. Guy wanted to avoid as much direct contact with the spore as possible. That was where the danger lay.

Guy was sorely tempted by thoughts of retracing his steps and finding a safe place to sit things out until the next day. He could always rejoin the company and report that the Indians had gotten too far ahead for him to catch up with them. It would be reasonable conduct under the circumstances of having been ordered to perform a duty specifically designed to get him killed.

But a man who came into his adulthood as a soldier had specific values and honor. A military man was hired by the state to risk his life. No matter how stupid, self-centered, or useless the orders from a superior officer were, the professional fighting man was required by law and custom to obey them. It was part of the oath of enlistment, and Sgt. Guy DuBose was unable to go back on his word.

He pressed on into the danger.

Guy took advantage of every rise the plains country offered him, no matter how slight. He rode onto these small mounds and stopped. Then he would stand up in the saddle, looking as far as possible in hopes of seeing some sign of the Chogolas that would warn him of what direction death could come from.

Finally, late in the afternoon, the hell he expected broke loose.

Ten Chogola Comanche warriors, shrieking in murderous delight, broke over the horizon to his right rear. Guy pulled his horse around to face them. He raised the carbine and took careful aim. A slow, precise squeeze on the trigger made the weapon buck in recoil. Its heavy slug sped across the expanse of prairie and lifted one Indian off his horse, ripping bone and muscle as the man crumpled to the dusty grass.

Now Guy violently wheeled his mount and fled in the opposite direction. He rode without panic, almost methodically, as the ground sped by beneath the hooves of his horse. It was awhile before he was aware the pursuers were firing at him. A couple of spurts of dirt ahead showed where wayward bullets struck the ground.

Guy set up a zigzagging course to make himself as difficult a target as possible. He turned a bit in the saddle for a look behind and saw that the smaller, swifter Indian horses were gaining on him. He stopped trying to dodge bullets, now concentrating on speed.

"Hay-yaaah!" he yelled at his horse and whistled *Charge*. The animal recognized the notes and galloped harder. It had spent countless afternoons going through cavalry maneuvers signaled by bugle calls. Instinctively, as if in line with its fellow mounts, the horse's excitement grew.

The chase went down a gentle draw and up the other side. Another glance informed Guy that the Indians were even closer but at least were not making any attempts at surrounding him. He gently tugged on the reins to slant off toward the south where the rest of Company C had to be.

The horse tossed its head and slowed. A fine spray of blood came out of its nostrils and spread over Guy's face. One of the Indians' bullets had finally found its mark. The brave animal stumbled and went down throwing the rider over its front. Guy hit the ground and came up instinctively pulling his pistol from the holster. He turned in time to see a coup stick slashing at him. He fired and heard a wild yell.

Another Indian came in shouting. He was followed by yet one more Chogola from a different angle. Guy fired frantically, but was bowled over by a third warrior. Again he hit the ground, but this time he could not get up. Dizzy and stunned, Guy tried to rise. Then he felt himself being pulled, rolled over, and his boots removed. Some more tusseling followed and when his head cleared, he was wearing only his longjohns. Cruel

217

ropes of rawhide bit into the flesh of his arms. Another was around his neck, leading to a mounted warrior.

"Hello, Rides-All-Day." The Chogola was one that Guy knew. A particularly nasty individual named Kicking Deer.

Guy grimaced but said nothing.

He knew three of the remaining eight. Two Ponies, Old Bow, and Young Buffalo grinned at him. Guy expected to be beaten to death for killing the Indian with the coup stick, but the Comanches only crowded around him with their horses forcing him to jump around in the stickers on his bare feet as he dodged the animals.

"Where is He-Whips-Them?" Young Buffalo asked.

"I don't know him," Guy answered.

"He is your chief," Young Buffalo said. "Remember when he told the other soldier to whip me?"

"Yes," Guy answered realizing that Blackburn had been given a well-deserved name by the Indians. He nodded his head toward the southern horizon. "He and all the other soldiers are over there. Very close. They will be here soon."

Two Ponies laughed. "That a lotta shit."

"You'll see," Guy said stubbornly.

"We go," Old Bow said. He turned and started off at a trot.

Guy, attached to Kicking Deer, had to follow on the run. Rocks, more stickers, and other debris on the ground quickly cut into his soft feet. He had no choice but to trot briskly. If he fell there would be no mercy shown. The Indian would drag him until his head separated from his body.

They passed the dead Indian who had failed to count

coup. Now Guy understood why the Chogolas weren't infuriated by his death. The corpse was that of a Kiowa. The man had probably been a visitor in Lame Elk's camp and had attached himself to this particular war party to experience a few thrills.

Guy's breathing became more difficult as the noose tightened around his neck. He had to open his mouth to suck in as much air as possible. His leg muscles ached with fatigue, but were forced to greater effort when the sergeant was led across gullies or up and down knolls.

Young Buffalo laughed and rode around the group. Now and then he would ride up to Guy and let his horse nudge the soldier enough to almost knock him off balance.

"Yah! Rides-All-Day! I change your name to Runs-All-Day!" He laughed at his joke and his companions joined in with their own approval of his humor. This encouraged Young Buffalo. "What you think, Runs-All-Day?" He bumped him again with the horse. "What, Runs-All-Day? You don't want talk with me?"

Guy paid no attention to the taunting. His mind raced with plans for escape. There was a limited time before the Indians would begin a long, slow execution. They liked mutilating their enemies alive even more than after death.

Life with Pauline seemed even farther away than it had been in the Yankee prison camp.

CHAPTER 20

The hidden Indians fired random, scattered shots at the soldiers. The Chogolas were situated in a large grove of mixed trees that grew along a waterway they called Crazy Woman Creek.

The small waterway had gotten its name years before when a captive white woman, whose husband had been tortured and killed by the tribe, went insane following the incident. Shrieking and laughing wildly, she had lived along its banks for several weeks before finally succumbing to starvation and exposure. The Indians, who thought insane persons were under the influence of strong spiritual medicine, named the creek to honor her.

Now the natural vegetation of the area gave the Indians good cover, making it almost impossible for them to be seen by the troopers facing them. The battle had been going on for more than two hours.

Early in the fight, Blackburn had ordered Company C to dismount. One trooper in every five had taken charge of his own horse and four others. These handlers moved back with the animals out of harm's way while the other four cavalrymen were on the skirmish line trading ineffectual shots with the concealed Indians.

Blackburn had also given the order to fire at will. Now he squatted a few yards to the rear with Morris Kramer at his side. Kramer, excited and interested, alternated between his notepad and taking exhilarated glances around. "By God, Gordon, this is the best I've seen since I got out here."

The captain was not in as good a mood. "What the hell are you talking about, Morris? We're just sitting here trading shots with the savage bastards."

"I know," Kramer agreed. "But the other occasions have been more running than fighting. This time you're really down eye-to-eye with those Indians."

"And getting nowhere," Blackburn complained. "They are snug and comfy in those God damned trees, while my men have only rare and poor targets to try and hit. Hell's bells! We don't even know how many of them are in that damned grove. This may not be much of a story either."

"Think not, old man? Would you care to see my scribblings?" Kramer asked.

Blackburn sighed. "I suppose I've nothing better to do in a situation like this." He took the notepad and read it. As he perused the story, he broke into a smile. "I didn't realize that my classic tactics, based on Napoleon's campaigns, had cornered the brutes here."

Kramer smiled back. "Would you want me to pen the absolute truth and write that you accidentally stumbled on them camped in those trees?"

"Not really, old man. That wouldn't do my career

much good," Blackburn answered.

"Nor mine," Kramer echoed.

They were interrupted by the arrival of Sgt. Harry Tate. "By your leave, sir," Tate greeted. "How long're we gonna keep this up?"

"Christ, Sergeant!" Blackburn exclaimed. "Until we defeat those sons of bitches!"

"Well, sir, begging your pardon, but we're not too far from the Red River Agency now," Tate said. "Me and Donovan has noticed that there's a whole passel o' women and kids in with a few warriors there. They was prob'ly on their way back when we stumbled across 'em."

"So?" Blackburn asked with a shrug.

"We figger them warriors is trying to get back to the agency to dump off their families, sir. Remember what Sergeant DuBose said? They've did this afore. When the weaker ones is safe and sound, the men will head back to the warpath," Tate said. "If we pulled back and let 'em outta them trees, we could git there before they do and have some more troops out from Fort Alexander to round 'em up."

"I see," Blackburn said. "Thank you very much for your counsel, Sergeant Tate. I shall take it under serious consideration."

"Yes, sir." Tate hurried away to rejoin his section.

"I don't like that," Morris Kramer said.

"What's the matter?" Blackburn asked. "Couldn't you write up a story as to how this military genius drove the savages into the arms of waiting troops?"

"But they'd get the glory, Gordon," Kramer protested. "You've got to defeat these Indians to make a real impression. I can only create so much. There are always official reports to take into consideration. We need to have you be the lone commander here."

Blackburn was thoughtful for a few seconds. "You're right." He called out, "Trumpeter Pullini! Front and center!"

The young Italian bugler appeared out of the grass. "Yes, Captain, sir?"

"Sound *Recall,* then follow up immediately with *To Horse,*" Blackburn ordered.

Pullini quickly complied. The troops answered the calls by forming up and moving backward. Then, with Sergeant Tate and the corporals directing, they proceeded to their horses and mounted up in the familiar column formation.

Blackburn, now in the saddle too, rode to the head of his command. "Company!" he ordered. "Sections form line to the front, march!"

Morris Kramer quickly cantered to the rear as the troops went through the maneuver. He turned, ready to use his well-trained observer's eye to take in the drama that was about to be played out on that clump of prairie country.

Now Company C was strung out in one long line facing the Indians in the small clump of woods. The troops were just over the horizon, out of sight of the Chogolas, as they dressed to the right and closed up until they were within arms reach of each other.

"Draw pistols!" Blackburn shouted. "Trumpeter! Sound the *Charge!*"

"*Immediatamente, Signore Capitano!*"

The abrupt, compelling notes of the most aggressive of bugle calls burst out over the command. Company C's horses leaped forward as the men leaned toward the front, their pistols held in outstretched hands.

The earth shook with the pounding of the forty-five sets of hooves. Many of the men cheered as the excitement in the company streaked upward toward a high pitch. When they bounded over the high ground and could see the trees that concealed the Chogolas, the firing broke out up and down the line of charging cavalrymen.

The Indians increased their fire, experiencing good luck at the massive target that loomed toward them in increasing speed. Several troopers pitched from their saddles, but their comrades pressed on.

The Indian women and children fled to the rear while their men defiantly and bravely stood their ground. The firing increased and so did the amount of casualties the soldiers sustained.

Harry Tate now took over. "Holster them pistols!" he roared over the musketry. "Dismount by squads and draw carbines!"

Once again the troopers went back to the routine of one soldier in five holding his friends' horses.

"As skirmishers!" Tate ordered. "Move out!"

Now, more careful with the single-shot Springfields, the men advanced by bounds taking advantage of the cover offered by the grass and dents in the ground. They moved rapidly until the shooting finally peaked, then dropped off sharply. As the soldiers moved into the trees they could see the sprawled corpses of five Chogolas. All bore several massive wounds inflicted by the large caliber army weapons.

"They're running out the other side of the trees," a trooper yelled.

A companion echoed his shout with, "Them Injuns is

headed straight for the agency!"

"Cease fire!" Harry Tate bellowed as several men shot at the disappearing sight of the fleeing Chogolas. He quickly sought out Captain Blackburn. The officer, who had stayed in the saddle, was easy to find. "Sir, the Redskins have flown the coop. I reckon that's that. They'll be snug as bugs under Palmer Druce's nose within another hour."

"God damn it!" Blackburn swore. "Fine, Sergeant. Get the men assembled and stand fast for further orders."

"Yes, sir," Tate said saluting. He trotted off yelling, "Pullini! Sound *Recall* and *Assembly!*"

Now Morris Kramer rode through the woods and joined his friend. "Did I hear right, Gordon? Did those Indians head for the safety of the agency?"

"I am afraid so," Blackburn said dejected.

"They can't do that," Kramer said in a worried tone.

Blackburn slowly shook his head. "There is not a damned thing I can do about it. We'll never be able to catch them or cut them off."

"Damn it all, Gordon!" Kramer said. "We've too good a thing going here to let it slip away."

Blackburn was angry. "What the hell do you want me to do, Morris? Attack the agency, for the love of God?"

"Yes!" Morris was insistent. "You fought the savages from the open plains back to the very government agency that had given them safety and sustenance. The ungrateful wretches attempted to kill the agent and his wife, but you rode to the rescue just in time. Do you hear me, Gordon? Just in time!" He looked meaningfully at his army friend. "Damn it all, man! Do you want to get back to the War Department or not?"

Blackburn grinned at the newspaperman. "Right." He swung his horse and galloped over to the assembled company. "Form up in columns," he yelled. "This fighting isn't over yet. Those Indians are off to attack the agency."

Sergeant Harry Tate was astounded. "No, sir! No, sir! They're leaving them women and kids there, then the warriors will skiddadle into the open country."

"Shut up, Sergeant!" Blackburn yelled in a fury. "We are going to ride to the rescue. Now hear me for the last time. Form up in columns!"

"Yes, sir," Tate replied. "Comp'ny, column of twos to the left, march!"

The outfit quickly formed up. Within a couple of minutes they rode out into the wide prairie terrain. Blackburn looked back at them. "Gallop, ho!" he commanded.

The pace picked up considerably.

The short trek took less than a half hour before the buildings and lodges at the agency were in view. Once again, mounted with pistols drawn, Company C awaited the orders to attack.

When he received the word, Pullini did not hesitate. He blew *Charge*. The men surged forward again, the rage and excitement of the previous fighting still hot in their blood.

There was general disorder among the Indians at the agency. The new arrivals had been greeted happily by their relatives and friends who had stayed behind rather than follow Lame Elk out on the warpath.

Talks-To-Them tried to calm everyone down. He was worried about the seven warriors who had also

227

entered the camp. "Why do you come here?" he demanded. "The soldiers at Fort Alexander will come and arrest you."

The leading warrior, an exhausted but unconquered fighter named Big Stag, pointed outward. "Hear me, Talks-To-Them. We had no choice. The soldiers chased us here from Crazy Woman Creek. We wanted to lead them out into the grasslands, but we feared for our families."

"Then you must leave now," Talks-To-Them said. "This is a time for using words against the white soldier chief instead of bullets."

"That soldier chief who chases us is He-Whips-Them," Big Stag replied. "He likes to see us suffer."

"Perhaps Rides-All-Day will calm his anger," Talks-To-Them suggested.

But Big Stag shook his head. "I fought those soldiers for a long time. I saw them all. Not once did I put my eyes on Rides-All-Day."

Talks-To-Them sighed. "Then it is time for wisdom and dealing. I will do it."

A cry from the outer edges of the agency abruptly sounded. "Soldiers! Soldiers!"

Talks-To-Them hurried toward the disturbance as fast as his ancient legs would carry him. People fled past him, running in the opposite direction. They had fearful expressions on their faces. "What is the matter?" he asked them. "Have you not seen the soldiers before?"

A woman, disheveled in her fear, looked at the old man. Her eyes were wide with panic. "They have come to kill us!"

"Foolish woman!" Talks-To-Them said. But he increased his pace. As he reached the outer lodges, the aged Indian could see the long line of soldiers rushing toward him. Talks-To-Them could also hear the bugle. He knew that song of the white soldiers. It meant they were angry beyond speaking. But he also realized he must try to bring some sort of control over the situation. The chief hurried around the last lodge and walked out a few yards into the open country.

A half-dozen of the .45 caliber slugs hit him almost simultaneously. The wiry oldster was whipped around like a puppet on a string as the force of the impact blew his life away.

Several cavalry mounts trampled his body as Company C continued the charge through the lodges. Dozens of these buffalo-skin affairs collapsed in the dust of the galloping troopers. Now, beyond control, the soldiery caught up with the Indians fleeing toward the protection of the agency buildings.

Big Stag and several of the men made a valiant, useless stand. Unable to find proper cover, they held their ground in an uneven line, firing as fast as they could into the attackers. The warriors died like Talks-To-Them, splattered by bullets before being smashed to pulp under the horses' hooves.

Wild but rapid fusillades swept through the crowd, bowling over the terrified women and children. A few old men threw their bodies at the lunging army mounts in vain attempts to slow them down and give the others a better chance to escape.

Finally, with a string of dead humanity spread out behind him, Capt. Gordon Blackburn signaled a halt.

The company, kicking clods and dust into the air, came to a staggering stop in the agency yard. Palmer and Netta Druce, in shock and disbelief, stared at the carnage around them.

Morris Kramer, who had drawn off to one side of the store, was writing rapidly in his notepad. The Battle of Crazy Woman Creek was over.

CHAPTER 21

Guy DuBose struggled with the rawhide bonds that squeezed hard into the flesh of his wrists and arms. He was exhausted and in a great deal of pain. But not all the acute physical discomfort he suffered was from leg cramps brought on by being forced to run behind Kicking Deer's horse.

Guy had barely been able to stand when his captors finally brought him to their camp. But his ordeal for that day was far from over. After being freed from his captors' tether, the Chogolas amused themselves by forcing him to run through their cookfire. A group on one side would push him into the flames; then after he leaped out others forced him back. They added to their fun by stabbing him with arrows, inflicting shallow but hurtful wounds.

Now, in the cool of the evening, he lay off to one side of the camp where the warriors had finally thrown him to wait until the next day. A lengthy death could be administered more properly then. The Chogolas ate the evening meal they prepared by themselves. There

231

were no women or children in the camp. Guy learned that they had been sent back to the Red River Agency with an escort of a few warriors. The Indian men knew that Palmer and Netta Druce would take care of their families while they continued their raiding activities.

Lame Elk himself had informed the soldier of the situation in haughty terms. "When they are safe with the Druce man and woman, the warriors will come back to us. Then we will raid in Texas and Kansas until the cold weather. After that we, too, will take the white man's road again and make friends with a treaty paper. Then we will eat his beef through the winter until next year's warring season."

Guy, listening to the boasts, could only hope that he would be alive the next year. From the continuing deterioration of the treatment he received, there was no doubt that the warriors meant to kill him. All the while that Lame Elk gloated at him about the band's intentions, Guy surveyed the camp. His initial sighting showed that the war band, including a dozen Kiowa guests, numbered over a hundred. There was no question that their attacks on isolated farms and ranches had been successful. The warriors sported fresh scalps and various bits of clothing and other loot. They were particularly fond of hats and vests. Many strode with their chests puffed out, dressed in those items of attire, sporting them as trophies of war.

"Am I your only captive?" Guy asked Lame Elk.

"We finish with the others," Lame Elk said. "They die slow like you tomorrow. We play with the womans, then hit them with clubs and throw them away."

Guy knew that any outward sign of anger or fear on his part would make things worse for him. He adopted

232

the Indians' attitude during captivity. He remained passive with an unexpressive face.

A young warrior was set to guard Guy. Now, separated a few yards from the main body of the war band, this Indian, bored with the job, amused himself by idly aiming his rifle at Guy's head now and then. Guy was careful to not so much as wince. It was another example of how any display of agitation or nervousness on his part would be met with shots when the game changed to seeing how close the Indian could come to hitting him.

Guy's feet were badly blistered from the torment he'd endured, and the bottoms of the legs on his army longjohn underwear were burned away. He worked against his bonds, noting that the ones around his wrist had begun to loosen slightly. After a half hour of effort, the slackness began to increase slightly. The problem was that Guy could only tend to this task when the young guard looked away.

A glance through the legs of the sentry showed him that the Indians had begun to drink. No doubt they had looted a wagonful of liquor during their marauding forays. One man, the alcohol hitting him the quickest, stood up and began singing a war song, shuffling through a dance. Others joined in until the Chogola version of a gala celebration was in full swing.

Now the guard's attention was on the festivities. The young man was almost frantic with a desire to get drunk and join the dance. Guy took advantage of the situation by working doubly hard with the slim straps on his wrist. It hurt like hell as his skin rubbed against the rawhide, but suddenly they parted with such abruptness that Guy was surprised to be free of them.

That left his ankles and the wrapping around his upper arms.

He would have been elated with this small bit of freedom, but Guy realized it would do him no good. Even if he were completely free of the leather restraints, escape would be impossible. In order to break loose, he would have to run to the hobbled Indian horses nearby, choose one and remove the bindings from the animal's fetlocks. If he hadn't been caught by then, he would have to leap up on its back and gallop away to freedom. All this while a hundred Indians, in the prime of life and athletic ability, would chase after him to put a stop to the escape. The only advantage he had was the fact that the Indians customarily kept the rawhide bridles on their horses. That way, the animals were always ready for pursuit or escape—whatever situation occurred in their camp.

The young guard moved with the rhythm of the dancers. He ached with a desire to go over to the celebration, but he was forbidden to do so. As an apprentice warrior, he had the most menial of camp chores to perform, including some that women normally tended to around the lodges. The celebration grew louder and drunker as the Chogolas and their Kiowa friends became more and more intoxicated.

Guy worked intermittently at the task all through the long night. The loud singing and celebrating did not let up. The effect of the liquor on the Indians maintained their activity at a high energy level. The continuous physical exertion of dancing kept complete intoxication at bay.

Dawn was easing into the darkness when Guy finally worked the rawhide around his arms up high enough that his elbows were relatively free. Each time his guard turned to look at him, the soldier would cease the activities, groaning and looking beaten down.

Suddenly a loud shout rose from the drinking, dancing crowd. A single warrior rode into their group. He was terribly agitated, shouting in a hoarse voice. After listening a few moments, Guy couldn't understand what the man said, but it was easy to tell the Chogola was weeping. He had brought some sort of terrible news. The other warriors began shouting in anger and grief, waving their rifles in the air.

Now the young Indian sentry's complete attention was given to the new arrival. Guy got to his feet, wincing against the awful pain. He hopped on his burnt feet, and pulled his arms out of the straps. There was so much shouting and yelling from the Indians that he didn't have to worry about noise. When he got up behind the youngster, Guy reached around and pulled his carbine from his grasp. The warrior, astonished and almost uncomprehending, whirled around.

Guy hit him hard, mustering every possible ounce of strength he could from his exhausted body. The butt of the weapon shattered the skull, striking with such force that one eyeball was knocked free from its socket. Guy didn't have time to marvel at the amount of strength his desperation had mustered in his punished body. He dropped down and dragged the Indian's knife from its scabbard. A couple of quick cuts and he was free from the other bonds.

The agony drove him to great speed as he rushed toward the Indians' herd of horses. Guy made no choice, he simply went to the nearest animal and slashed the hobble. The horse resisted a bit, but Guy

235

swung up on its back. He kicked hard in the ribs and slapped his newly acquired mount.

The shouts of frenzied Chogola Comanches and Kiowas echoed through the early morning air as Guy DuBose made his desperate try for freedom and a return to Pauline.

CHAPTER 22

The sun pounded down on the open prairie country like an invisible hammer slamming onto an anvil. Heat waves danced across the horizon, obscuring vision with shimering images. Capt. Gordon Blackburn could barely make out the sight of a figure riding toward him and the other troops.

"Guidon bearer," he called. "Can you see who that is?"

"Yes, sir," Pvt. Paddy McNally answered. He could see the hulking way in which the man sat his horse. "That'd be Donovan, sir."

Blackburn watched the man draw closer. "Ah, yes! So it is."

Five minutes later, the burly Irishman reined up beside Company C's commanding officer. "Sir, Private Donovan beggin' to report in from scout. There's a large group o' Injuns to the north, sir. I'm thinkin' they number thirty."

"Well, we've a few more men than that," Blackburn said. "What say we run the devils off and kill a few like

237

we did back at the agency?"

"Beggin' yer pardon, sir," Donovan said. "But I wouldn't jump into nothin' like that."

Anger flashed out of Blackburn's eyes. "Don't give me advice, Private Donovan! I've yet to seek counsel from the lower enlisted ranks during all my years in the army."

"I'm sorry, sir," Donovan said in apology. "I thought it was my duty as scout."

"Your reconnaissance assignments mean that you tell me only what you have seen. I do not care a whit about your tactical decisions."

"Yes, sir. It won't happen again, sir."

"See that it doesn't, by God!" Blackburn said. "Return to your place in the column."

Donovan rode back to the line of troopers passing Sgt. Harry Tate, who had pulled out to approach the captain. "By yore leave, sir. I really think you oughta give the matter some careful thinking."

Blackburn laughed. "You too, Sergeant Tate?" He leaned toward Morris Kramer. "Have you got all that, Morris? Be sure and write that the men of Company C have lost their stomach for fighting."

Tate's face reddened. "No, sir. Not a'tall. But I think we'd best take a few more looks around afore we light out in any attack."

Blackburn was surprised at Tate's boldness. Usually the sergeant took orders and displayed no less than blind trust and obedience. "Really, Sergeant Tate. Did we hesitate like this at the Red River Agency?"

"They was mostly women and kids there, sir," Tate protested. "They wasn't more'n a warrior or two amongst the dead men. The rest was old codgers."

Blackburn spoke softly, baring his teeth in a snarl. "If I ever hear you speak of that incident in such a manner, I shall hound you down to the rank of private, Tate. Is that what you want?"

Tate was angry about Guy DuBose. "O'course not, sir. But there's been real strange things going on in this patrol."

"Return to your section," Blackburn said. He watched the sergeant turn away and rejoin the column. "Trumpeter!"

Trumpeter Benito Pullini came forward. "Yes, sir, Captain?"

"Stick close to me," Blackburn said. "I will be needing your musical talents to direct this battle."

"Yes, sir."

Within moments, the company galloped northward toward the spot where Donovan spotted the crowd of hostiles. They rode confidently. Capt. Gordon Blackburn leaned over and slapped Morris Kramer on the shoulder. "This should wrap it up nicely, old man. I hope that when we are once again settled in the capital, you will be over to our house for tea the first chance you get."

"Delighted!" Kramer responded. "May I extend an early welcome back to Washington City society?"

Down the line, young Ben Horn, beside his new friend big Tim Donovan, glanced at his pal and winked. Donovan grinned back, but his eyes were serious. The veteran Irish soldier had bad feelings. For the first time he had sensed the "evil eye" in Captain Blackburn. According to the legends of the old country, that meant terrible luck for everyone.

Up forward from Donovan and Horn, ex-corporal

Hansen, still a private for his unauthorized rescue attempt of the fallen trooper, was looking right at Sgt. Harry Tate. Hansen was worried. "How does it look then, Sergeant Tate?"

Tate, remaining silent, only shook his head.

Up at the front of the column, riding behind Blackburn and Kramer, Paddy McNally, with Trumpeter Benito Pullini as a partner, kept the guidon's staff straight and true while the small flag that identified the company letter and regimental number fluttered proudly.

They cantered over the gently rolling terrain for a quarter of an hour before the Indians were sighted. Donovan had been right. They numbered about thirty. Blackburn drew his pistol and stood up in his stirrups.

"Do you see them, men?" he shouted. "One more grand victory! Follow me!"

The Chogolas and Kiowas stayed on the horizon traveling from east to west. Blackburn, with his men strung out behind him in a long line, cut sharply in an attempt to shorten the angle between himself and the fleeing Indians. He rode hard now, feeling the horse pounding wildly over the thick grass carpet of the prairie.

"For the love o'God, sir!" Sgt. Harry Tate's voice went unheard over the pounding of the hooves.

Blackburn caught a movement off to his left. He looked hard, seeing another group of about thirty hostiles. They were riding toward him. Now, too, were the original bunch who had turned. Fear and alarm streaked through his soul. He pulled hard on the reins, going back to the right. But now a third band was charging toward him and his command.

Then another smaller one, then another, and another.

Now Blackburn panicked. He damned convention and military tradition. The only thing he had on his mind was getting the hell away from that area as quickly as possible. He made a one hundred and eighty degree turn with his troops following. Frantic glances showed him that the Indians were closing in fast.

Sgt. Harry Tate forced his horse into a greater effort. He reached Pullini, yelling across to him. "Sound *Halt,* God damn you, Eye-talian. And do it now!"

Pullini sounded the single C-note of the call several times. The unit came to a sloppy, milling finish of the ride.

"Dismount, boys," Tate yelled in near uncontrolled fear and excitement. "Rally to me!"

Company C formed a circle with their backs to the interior, crowding in with carbines bristling outward. Inside, as Tate began to direct the firing, Blackburn and Kramer stood shoulder to shoulder.

"My God!" Blackburn cried.

Kramer, forgetting his notepad, said nothing. He simply looked at what was going on through wide-opened eyes.

The Indians, now over a hundred strong, bellowed and sang their war chants as they charged down on the little group of soldiers.

CHAPTER 23

Guy DuBose could not figure out why there was no pursuit after his escape. His apprehensive looks to his rear as he fled for his life revealed nothing. Even at the outset of his dash for freedom after he'd clubbed his guard, Guy made no effort to sneak quietly away once he was on the Indian horse.

The soldier damned noise discipline as he gave the eager animal its head and allowed it to gallop as madly as it wanted out of the camp. He continued to give in to the mount's eagerness to run as long as it moved southward.

When he'd gone a great distance, he finally forced the animal to control its exuberance. Riding that fast for a long length of time would exhaust the horse—and it was dangerous. The plains country held prairie dog holes and other natural traps in which a horse's leg could easily be broken.

Finally, when glances all around told him the near countryside was empty, Guy took advantage of the situation. He came to a complete halt to simply wait and listen. He wanted to find out for sure from which direction the Chogolas were chasing him.

But there was nothing but the sounds of chirping, whirring insects making their mating sounds in the warm morning. That was a sure sign that no human lurked through the grass toward him. Puzzled, but relieved, Guy resumed his escape at a slower, surer pace. Only then, after the initial excitement died off, did he notice the growing pain in his burned feet, hanging down on each side of the animal. As the blood collected in them, the hurt began to pulsate in time to his heartbeat. All he could do was try to ignore the torment even as it grew worse.

The rest of the morning was a whirl of nervous stops and starts. Still unable to believe he had gotten away clean, Guy spent more time simply listening. Weaponless, except for the knife he'd taken from the Indian he'd killed, the veteran soldier knew that there was no way he could keep any adversaries at bay for much time.

Mid-day arrived bright and hot, casting brilliant sunlight over a prairie that was empty save for Guy, his horse, and the assorted creatures who made that part of the country their home. Now, damning caution, he pressed on, trusting in luck and his eyesight. His feet were badly swollen, and he knew that if he didn't reach help within the next twenty-four hours, irreparable infection would set in.

He finally found some brackish water in a buffalo wallow. He drank the muddy liquid carefully, trying to keep as much silt out of his mouth as possible. With his thirst barely satisfied, he went on. The sun was much hotter a couple of hours later. He knew it was burning im badly, but there was nothing he could do about it. Finding shade and staying there until early evening would only make him vulnerable to discovery.

Guy heard the massive shooting later in the afternoon. He recognized the heavy "pows" of Springfield carbines interspersed with much more numerous "pops" of other weapons. The army weapons encouraged him enough that he damned all caution and moved toward the sound of the fighting. If cavalrymen and Indians were engaged in battle, Guy figured the soldiers would win.

It was over amazingly quick. But Guy pinpointed the exact direction toward the short-lived fighting by noting a hazy grove of trees on the southern horizon. They were straight in the direction that led toward the battle site. Trusting in pure luck, he pressed on hoping to find some of Fort Alexander's troops at the end of the agony.

Seeing at any distance at all was difficult. Guy perceived dancing blobs ahead of him. They rose and fell back to the ground in graceful swoops. His sun-eaten mind could not muddle through the effort of figuring out what they were. But finally, he realized they were large birds.

As he drew closer to them he could hear their caws, and recognized them as crows. Then he could see what attracted them to the area. Naked bodies, impaled by arrows, lay close together. Guy, dreading what he must see, rode on until he reached the awful place. Now the buzzing of flies over the cadavers could be heard among the birds' excited calls.

Scalped, hacked, and slashed open, Company C answered its last muster. Guy could see what was left of

Paddy McNally, the shaft of his beloved guidon driven through his disemboweled stomach. Trumpeter Pullini, face up, had a calm expression on his Italian countenance even if his head had been chopped from his body. Ben Horn and Tim Donovan had died and were mutilated, side-by-side as soldier comrades, while ex-Corporal Hansen was scattered in several parts at their feet.

A quick shock of grief hit Guy when he saw the remains of his faithful friend Sgt. Harry Tate. Now Martha would be alone with the children, forced to leave Fort Alexander. The army had little use for the widows and orphans of dead soldiers. It was cruel, but Lt. Joseph Harris as adjutant and Lt. Bill Robertson as quartermaster would have no choice but to follow regulations and have her moved off Soap Suds Row and the military reservation.

Guy rode around the camp until he could see Morris Kramer. The newspaperman's notes, torn up and scattered, were soaking in his blood. Guy swung his eyes to the center of the pile and saw Capt. Gordon Blackburn, just a head and crow-bitten torso, with the arms and legs severed and thrown away someplace. Every member of the command had been scalped. Those parts of them were now trophies of war, proudly displayed by Chogola Comanche and Kiowa fighting men.

Now Guy realized where his potential pursuers had been. The messenger who arrived in their camp must have told them of the company's location. Guy, who knew nothing of the massacre of Chogola oldsters, women, and children at the Red River Agency, thought that Lame Elk had decided to go for the chance to kill many soldiers, rather than chase one who had escaped the camp.

Guy turned his horse south and rode away from the butchery.

The remainder of the day merged into a hodge-podge of blistering heat from the sun, dry hot wind, and the torment of his feet. As his lucidness failed, Guy's last sensation was that of his right foot. It had swollen so much that the flesh had burst.

Time was no longer a dimension in his life. Hallucination and blessed unconsciousness ran in and out of his awareness. Guy's eyelids were swollen almost shut. The sun had burned him badly, making even his lips blister. Dried out and dangerously dehydrated, he remained aboard the horse through sheer instinct.

A wavy view of sky and grass came into focus now and then. At one point he could see Inez, the Druce's Mexican housekeeper, looking at him. Her eyes were wide and she seemed to be screaming in terror. The light faded and he went back into the troubled dreamland of his whirling mind.

Other pictures broke in now and then. Soldiers, Netta Druce and her husband, and even Pauline. The regimental surgeon and chaplain also made appearances as his mental state cleared little by little.

Finally Guy could clearly see Pauline smiling down at him. Although groggy, he became more and more aware of his surroundings. He was on a bed in the post hospital, and she was sitting on a chair beside him.

Guy licked his dry lips, feeling the punished skin. He struggled to speak, "How long—"

"You've been back almost two weeks," Pauline said. "The Druces said you rode into the agency. They

247

brought you to the post."

"Oh, my—" Then he saw Minnie Robertson standing behind her.

Pauline reached out and lay a cool hand on his face. She bent down and kissed his cheek. "It's all right, darling. Everyone knows about us now."

EPILOGUE

Dan Wayne, Captain, United States Cavalry, Retired, straightened his cravat, then slipped into his jacket. He checked his reflection in the hallway mirror of his spacious Dallas, Texas home. After adjusting the carnation in his lapel, he took another look. Dan liked what he saw.

Six months of sobriety had taken the puffiness out of his face, turning its former pallor healthy pink. Dan Wayne looked a hell of a lot healthier than he had in at least ten years. Particularly those final ones spent at Fort Alexander as an alcoholic company commander with more interest in the bottle than his soldiers.

Much had happened to the old soldier since his retirement from the army a bit over a year previously. He'd gone into a land development business with his brother in Dallas. The enterprise, which was on solid footing to begin with, had grown even more profitable. Dan, his staff and command experience helping a great deal, proved to a valuable addition to the firm. But for awhile, the ex-captain followed the routine of his old army life: He worked hard and steady, while drinking harder and faster. It looked for awhile like he'd coast on down to a relatively early death, and leave his money to his nephews and nieces.

But then he met Emma Meadows.

She was a wealthy widow whose husband had worked with Dan's brother on several deals. Dan, when introduced to her at a Sunday social, found her a buxom, attractive woman. At first she was quite distant and cold to him due to his dedication to liquor. His reputation as a *bon vivant* around the best of the city's saloons was well known. When his premier efforts at establishing a rapport of sorts were rebuffed, he decided to sober up a bit and see what would happen in their relationship.

What happened was that Dan Wayne quit the bottle and got married.

The ancient cavalryman liked the life. A sensible wife to keep him on the straight and narrow was just what he needed. They both prospered by using Dan's new business connections and growing bank account with her considerable money. True, Dan Wayne got a lot thicker around the waist than he had been in his cavalry days, but physically and mentally he was in much better shape.

Now, slipping the jaunty derby on his head, he turned and walked to the front door where Emma awaited to bid him goodby. "I'm off, my dear," Dan said. "It looks like another brisk turn of business today."

Emma smiled and kissed him. "Don't be late for supper. Olivia promised us roast beef and pinto beans."

"Mmm! I can taste it already," Dan said returning

the kiss. "Until later, my love." He went through the door, crossed the immense front porch of his large home and walked down to the curb where his carriage waited.

"Good morning, Cap'n Wayne," the driver greeted.

Everyone insisted on using his old army rank. It was really Emma's idea, so he didn't mind, although sometimes he wished his military career had been successful enough that he could be called "Major" or even "Colonel."

"Good morning, Ed," Dan greeted as he bounded up into the passenger's seat with a springy step.

The horse and carriage clacked off down the bricked road of Dallas' most exclusive residential section. They went around a corner and down two blocks as they always did. When Ed brought the vehicle to a halt, Dan got out and crossed the sidewalk to enter a gate. He went up to the front door of the house there and pulled on the bell.

The door was opened by a maid dressed in starched white and somber black. "Good morning, Cap'n Wayne," she greeted. "Please to come in, sir."

"Thank you, Mrs. Tate," he said cheerfully. When he'd left Fort Alexander, he had never expected to see Sergeant Tate's wife again, especially as a widow. "I assume they're at the breakfast table."

"Yes, sir," Martha Tate said. "And waitin' for you as usual."

"I know the way," Dan said. He visited the home on almost a daily basis. He went into the dining room. "Hello! Hello!" he said.

Guy DuBose pulled his watch from its place in his trouser pocket. "Oh! Sorry, Dan. I didn't know it was so late."

"Quite all right," Dan said. "There's no rush this morning."

Pauline DuBose smiled at him. "Would you care for a cup of coffee, Dan? Martha will fetch you one."

"Don't mind if I do, my dear," Dan said. He glanced at Guy. "Go ahead and read your paper."

"I'm almost finished with this article," Guy said. "It's most interesting. Lame Elk and several of his warriors are being sent to prison in Florida."

"Mmm," Dan mused. "No more resting between raids eating government beef at the Red River Agency, hey?"

"I guess not," Guy said. "As a matter of fact, he never returned there after the—" He glanced around to see if Martha Tate was close by. Guy always avoided speaking of the massacre of Company C where Harry Tate had died if she were near. "As I was saying, Lame Elk stayed on the run after what happened to the company. He was finally brought in a couple of weeks before my discharge from the army. The government has been trying to decide what to do with him since." He folded the newspaper and set it aside. "Those Chogolas will die in prison, of course. If being caged doesn't do it, then the Florida weather will."

Martha Tate came in the dining room with a fresh pot of coffee. She poured a cup for Dan. "I can remember when Mister DuBose and my men drank this stuff with sutler's whiskey in it."

"I do too," Guy said smiling.

"Say!" Dan said suddenly remembering. "We've got a wedding to go to Sunday, don't we?"

"Yes," Martha said smiling. "I'm so glad Laura Lee

252

ain't marrying no soljer." She gazed fondly at the people seated around the table. "And we're plumb honored y'all are attending."

"We're one family, Martha," Guy said. "We grew close under very trying circumstances."

"That's for sure, Mister DuBose," Martha said. "If anybody wants more coffee, just sing out." She left the room.

Dan was deep in thought for several moments. "It's strange, but, even after fighting them for years and what happened to my friends in Company C, I never developed a passionate hatred toward the Indians."

"They were defending themselves," Guy said. "It's the old historical adage. They had something that some other group of people wanted who were stronger and more numerous—the Indians' land."

Pauline, with the personal tragedies of the Civil War as fresh in her heart as when they happened, nodded sadly. "Perhaps the day will come when we mortals will be able to overcome our problems without war."

"I doubt that," Guy said. He and Pauline had been married shortly after his release from military service. If her marriage so soon after her husband's death shocked anyone who knew about it, the couple didn't care. As far as Guy and Pauline were concerned, they had waited twelve long years. Any more passage of time in bringing their love to fulfillment seemed useless cruelty to themselves.

"I fear I must agree with your husband, Pauline," Dan said. "Man will continue fighting man to the end of this miserable planet's existence." He turned his glance toward Guy, noticing the cane hanging on the ex-sergeant's chair. "Has the new doctor been any help with your feet?"

"He certainly has," Guy said. "I'm lucky I didn't either lose them or die of gangrene. Some of the burns went pretty deep. I suppose I shall always limp a little. It can't be helped."

"Please!" Pauline said. "Let's talk about something else."

"Of course," Dan said kindly. He changed the subject. "I hear the merchant association is taking the north tract."

"I'm having the papers finalized today," Guy answered. "That will be a profitable little deal."

"Little—*little?*" Dan asked taking a healthy gulp from his cup of coffee. "Say, Guy! For a couple of former cavalry soldiers, you and I have been doing mighty good for ourselves with these Dallas slickers."

Guy nodded. "Yes. In another year we'll be right up there with them."

"We're almost there now," Dan said sipping the coffee. "By the way, are you going to hang on to those acres you picked up on the Saunders contract?"

"I had to take them as part of the agreement," Guy said. "And I don't think I'll be able to sell that land to anyone."

"I guess not," Dan said. "The ground there is reeking with all that petroleum gunk. Who wants that?"

Guy shrugged. "I wonder what my heirs will say when they inherit the deed."

Dan laughed. "They'll think ol' grandpa got took." He finished his coffee. "Ready to go?"

"Sure am," Guy said. He motioned to Pauline to sit down when she started to stand up. "I don't want you doing any unnecessary moving around in your condition."

Pauline sighed. "Guy, I didn't break a leg. I'm only having a baby."

"Just the same," he said. Guy, leaning a bit on the cane, limped around and got his goodby kiss. "See you tonight."

The two men made their way through the house to the door. Dan stopped on the steps and pointed to the clear, blue sky. "That's the sign that this year's summer is going to be a dandy."

"I'll tell you one thing," Guy said setting his hat on his head. "It'll be a hell of a lot better than last year."

Dan, knowing the full story of Guy's last months in the army, broke into loud laughter. "Come on, soldier-boy. Let's go make some money!"